"They're not here," Wanda said, as if she couldn't believe it.

"These boxes co _____ _____ *The Oakdale Chronicle* f___ _____ ___ith nothing in between,"

"The library was _____ ___ _____ _om 1933. Now they're mi___ng from here, too?" Joe asked in disbelief, as he looked around the *Chronicle*'s basement.

"Maybe the boxes containing 1933 are just out of sequence," Wanda said hopefully. "Kids, we need to check every box!"

Joe, David, Sam, and Wanda split up and began to examine the labels on each box. Wishbone stayed with Joe.

It didn't take long to examine every label in the archives. Unfortunately, the boxes containing the 1933 issues were still missing.

"This is a dark day for Oakdale," Wanda said dramatically. "As president of the Oakdale Historical Society, I declare this a national disaster!"

Books in the WISHBONE™ Mysteries series:

Books in the WISHBONE SUPER Mysteries series:

*coming soon

WISHBONE Mysteries

FORGOTTEN HEROES

by Michael Anthony Steele

WISHBONE™ created by Rick Duffield

Big Red Chair Books™, *A Division of **Lyrick Publishing**™*

Big Red Chair Books™, *A Division of Lyrick Publishing*™
300 E. Bethany Drive, Allen, Texas 75002

©1998, 1999 Big Feats! Entertainment

Edited by Kevin Ryan

Copy edited by Jonathon Brodman

Continuity editing by Grace Gantt

Cover concept and design by Lyle Miller

Interior illustrations by Al Fiorentino

Wishbone photograph by Carol Kaelson

Library of Congress Catalog Card Number: 98-84945

ISBN: 1-57064-761-5

First printing: October 1998

10 9 8 7 6 5 4 3 2 1

Editor's Note

Big Red Chair Books dedicates this book to all
the heroes of the Negro Baseball League, and,
in particular, the 1933 national champions—
the Chicago American Giants.

*Thanks to Kevin for the story, and for knowing I feel
just as strongly about baseball as he does*

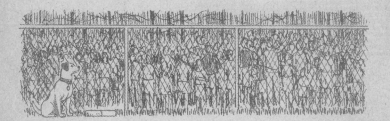

FROM THE BIG RED CHAIR . . .

Oh . . . hi! Wishbone here. You caught me right in the middle of some of my favorite things—books. Let me welcome you to the WISHBONE MYSTERIES. In each story, I help my human friends solve a puzzling mystery. In *FORGOTTEN HEROES*, Joe buys a shoe box full of valuable baseball cards at a garage sale. In researching the history of some of these cards, Joe—along with Sam, David, and me—discovers that some of our town's historical documents are missing. Will we find the records, or will part of Oakdale's history vanish forever?

The story takes place in the summer, just before the events that you'll see in the second season of my WISHBONE television show. In this story, Joe is fourteen, and he and his friends will be entering the eighth grade. Like me, they are always ready for adventure . . . and a good mystery.

You're in for a real treat, so pull up a chair and a snack and sink your teeth into *FORGOTTEN HEROES!*

Chapter One

C rack!!!

Wishbone watched as his best friend, Joe Talbot, swung his bat and hit an incredible fly ball high above center field. Wishbone, Joe, and their friends Samantha Kepler and David Barnes were all outside on a late Sunday afternoon hitting a few balls around Legion Field, an old, run-down ballpark on the north side of Oakdale.

Joe had hit the ball so hard that it headed toward the tall weeds that grew next to the far outfield. It could easily get lost there. Wishbone thought, *Lucky for Joe, Sam, and David that they happen to have one of the best outfielders in town—me!*

The little white-with-brown-and-black-spots dog raced off toward the spot where he knew the ball would land. As he ran, he kept an eye on the high-flying baseball. When the ball finally hit the ground just before the weeds, it bounced up. Wishbone leaped into the air and flew toward the rising ball. He opened his mouth wide and caught it between his teeth.

"Ha-ha!" The little dog laughed as his four paws hit the soil, and he set the ball down. "Caught it on the first bounce!"

Wishbone proudly picked up the ball in his mouth and ran back toward the pitcher's mound. He was ready to drop it off with David, who was pitching. Then he would head back out to catch the next ball. But as he approached the mound, he saw that the kids were packing up and preparing to leave the field. That was okay, too, he thought, as he looked toward the west. The summer sun was just beginning to dip down behind the distant treetops. From the looks of the sun and the growling in his stomach, it was definitely getting close to dinnertime.

Wishbone trotted over to where Joe, Sam, and David were picking up a few loose baseballs and stuffing them into their backpacks.

"That was a really good catch you just made, Wishbone," Joe told him.

Wishbone dropped the baseball into the fourteen-year-old boy's outstretched hand. Joe was wearing shorts and a brown T-shirt. Some of his short brown hair, damp with sweat, was stuck to his forehead. The rest ruffled in the soft, cool breeze that blew across the field.

"Hey," the Jack Russell terrier replied, "if you're not a good hitter, you've got to be a good fielder." Wishbone trotted over and lay down right on top of home plate. His tongue hung slightly out of his open mouth as panted.

"Are you two heading home?" Joe asked David and Sam.

"I'm going to the library," David replied. "I've got a little research to do."

Wishbone turned his head toward David. The dark, curly-haired boy was wearing blue jeans and a blue T-shirt. David Barnes was Oakdale's resident scientist-in-training. He was the kind of person who was always experimenting and trying to learn more about the world. His hunger for knowledge was almost as strong as Wishbone's hunger for adventure.

"It's back to work for me," Samantha Kepler added. "Sunday night can be pretty busy for us."

Speaking of snacks, Samantha, or Sam, as she was known by her friends, worked at one of Wishbone's favorite places in Oakdale—Pepper Pete's Pizza Parlor. She was another one of Wishbone and Joe's best pals. The blond-haired girl wore her hair pulled back in a ponytail. Sam had always been a good friend with a sense of adventure that was almost as big as Wishbone's. She was always the first person anyone could turn to for support. After her father, Walter Kepler, bought Pepper Pete's, she was also the first person Wishbone could turn to for a snack.

Wishbone's mouth watered just thinking about all those delicious pepperoni pizzas. A slice would really hit the spot right now. Of course, pizza would hit the spot almost *anytime* . . . okay, *all the time!* he thought.

"Okay," Joe replied. "I'll see you two later."

The three kids put on their safety helmets and got on their bikes. Sam and David took a shortcut across the field and headed for town. Joe sat on his bike and then he started to pedal for the nearby street that ran behind home plate. Wishbone immediately jumped to his feet.

"Come on, Joe!" Wishbone called as he leaped into motion. "I'll race you home!" The energetic dog ran off the baseball field, and Joe rode his bike close behind. When Wishbone's paws hit the sidewalk that ran in back of the field, he stopped and turned to see how far Joe was behind him.

He saw Joe pedaling his bike away from home plate and toward the street. His baseball glove was hanging from one handlebar, and his bat was resting across the bars.

Seeing that his pal wasn't far behind, the little dog took one last look at Legion Field. The field itself was quite large, but pretty messy. The infield was mostly dirt, with some large patches of grass. The outfield, which was surrounded by weeds, was mostly bordered by an old, falling-down wooden wall. Wishbone saw the area where the missing section of the wall was. Sam and David had ridden their bikes through the spot on their way back to the center of town.

Another feature of Legion Field was its stands. Behind home plate and the infield stood rows and rows of old, warped wooden bleacher seats that sat under an aging wooden press box. In front of the bleachers were two dugouts where loose planks from the walls hung over what once was the players' benches.

Everything about the field was run-down. Still, it had a certain beauty that was hard to describe. It was like an old chew toy that had been gnawed on so much that it was almost impossible to tell what it was anymore. Yet, the craving to chew on it still remained.

Usually, Joe, Sam, and David played ball at Jackson Park's clean, new baseball field. However, every now and then, Joe encouraged his friends to ride their bikes a little farther and play at old Legion Field. Joe said it had character.

Either way, the trip always meant a whole new set of smells for Wishbone to discover. After all, the dog and his friends didn't get over to the older part of Oakdale very often. All of the lingering scents there were a lot less familiar to him.

Wishbone took off down the street. His nose was to the ground so he could pick up some of the neighborhood news. A warm breeze ruffled his fur as Wishbone pushed his nose close to a small bush. He discovered one familiar scent, plus six new but similar smells all around the first one. It seemed that Jenny the Chow had a new litter of puppies. Wishbone lifted his head and turned back to see that Joe had almost caught up with him. The terrier dashed down the sidewalk to put a little more distance between them.

This was the way they usually traveled. Since Wishbone didn't have time to sniff out that *entire* part of town, he had to investigate the less-important smells with the casual sniff-by. But when he found something very interesting, Wishbone was usually far enough ahead of Joe so that he could stop and use both nostrils to check out the surrounding area.

As Wishbone ran down the sidewalk, he saw they were coming to a small intersection. Just as he was about to lower his nose to the base of the lamppost at the corner, the light breeze blew an even more interesting scent past his alert nose. Wishbone stopped, turned his head into the wind, and took a deep breath. It smelled like the inside of someone's house. Of course, it was always strange to smell the inside of someone's house from outside, mixed with all the other outdoor aromas. But Wishbone knew that it could mean only one thing—a yard sale!

Wishbone took a right down the intersecting street. Right away, two houses down, he spotted a large, old house. The house itself looked even older than Legion Field did. However, it was in a lot better condition.

Laid out in front of the house were blankets holding all sorts of household goods, and card tables full of all kinds of interesting items. Wishbone had to get a closer look—and a deeper sniff! After all, what better place could a dog get such a wide variety of scents? Even though dinnertime was coming up fast, a quick investigation could never hurt.

Behind him, Wishbone heard Joe calling his name.

"Don't worry, Joe," Wishbone replied. "Just a few quick sniffs and I'll catch up to you!"

Wishbone quickly made his way to the first blanket full of goodies. A bowling ball . . . *sniff* . . . an old lamp . . . *sniff* . . . a box of old records . . . *sniff, sniff*. On almost everything he sniffed, Wishbone noticed an interesting odor. It was the smell of another dog—a poodle, maybe. It was hard to tell, because the smell was so mild. It was as if the dog had not lived there in a long time.

Wishbone continued to go about his investigation: some pillows . . . *sniff* . . . some old shoes . . . *sniff* . . . —pew!—a box full of bubble-gum-smelling cards . . .

sniff . . . Hey! Wishbone stayed with the cards a bit longer. *Joe has a bunch of these bubble-gum-smelling cards,* Wishbone thought. *Maybe he'd like some more!* Wishbone turned to see that Joe had followed him down the street. He began to bark to get Joe's attention.

Joe noticed that Wishbone had stopped at a yard sale and seemed to have found something interesting. Joe heard Wishbone barking, but his mind wandered back to Legion Field. Now, *that* was a baseball field! The wooden bleachers, the old dugouts, the old advertisements on the back wall. The field was run-down, but it had a nostalgic feel that other fields didn't have. Joe had no idea why hardly anyone else ever used it, or why no one bothered to take care of it. He supposed that everyone would rather play at a nice new field like the one at the high school, or the one at Jackson Park. When Joe played ball at Legion Field, however, he could imagine himself being in the big leagues, under the eyes of a cheering crowd.

Wishbone barked again, bringing Joe out of his daydream. Joe reached the yard, propped his bike on its kickstand, and began to look around at the yard sale. There were two ladies standing close to the house. They seemed to be involved in a conversation about the quality and origin of a tall floor lamp. Without eavesdropping, it was hard to tell who the seller was and who the buyer was.

Joe turned his attention to the house behind them. It was a tall, two-story green house. It was trimmed in white and had a porch that wrapped around the front and one side of the house. To Joe, the house reminded him of the place where his next-door neighbor, Wanda Gilmore, lived. But this house was a bit bigger, and a lot less colorful. His eyes moved from the house to the many objects for sale.

All the items on sale were laid out in rows. As Joe began to walk down the first row, he heard Wishbone bark. He looked up to see his dog in front of a blanket full of stuff, barking at something on the ground. Joe quickly walked over.

"What have you found, boy?" Joe asked, kneeling beside Wishbone.

Joe ran a hand down Wishbone's back. Then he looked down to see an old shoe box—one that was stuffed with old baseball cards! Joe's eyes widened as he carefully picked up the old box.

"Way to go, Wishbone!" Joe said with excitement.

With great care, Joe began to flip through the cards. They were stacked tightly on their sides. As Joe looked at the cards, he saw many of the same years and team members he had in the collection he had inherited from his father, who had died when Joe was a little boy.

Incredibly, it seemed that there wasn't a card in the collection from after 1975, and most were in great condition. He even found player's cards from 1950s teams like the Brooklyn Dodgers and the Philadelphia Athletics. What an incredible find!

"*Ahem!*" someone said, making a throat-clearing sound.

Startled, Joe looked up to see one of the two ladies he had noticed a few minutes earlier. This one was the older of the two. She appeared to be in her late sixties. She wore a white dress with a pattern of small purple flowers on it. On her head was a purple, wide-brimmed hat.

"Did you find something you like?" the lady asked him.

"Uh . . . yes, ma'am," Joe replied, as he stood up, holding the box of cards. "I was wondering how much these cards cost."

The lady seemed about to answer, caught herself, then said, "What are your plans for them, young man?"

Joe was caught off guard by the question. "Excuse me?" he asked, thinking he might have misunderstood her.

"I mean," the lady continued, "do you plan on reselling these cards?" She pointed to the box in Joe's hands. "Or would you be thinking about trading them in for something else at a comic-book shop?"

"No, ma'am," Joe quickly replied. "That's probably the last thing I'd do." Joe looked down at the cards, then back at the woman. "You see, my father used to collect baseball cards. After he died, I tried to keep adding to his collection." Joe saw a smile appear on the woman's face. He guessed he'd given her the answer she was hoping for. He continued: "I've already seen a few cards in here that I know could fill some of the gaps in the collection that my dad left to me."

The lady didn't say anything at first. Instead, she looked toward the street. Joe followed her gaze to where his bicycle was parked on the sidewalk. The baseball glove that hung from the handlebar swayed slightly in the late-day breeze.

Wishbone let out a small, gruff bark and pawed Joe's leg. Both Joe and the yard sale's owner turned their attention to the terrier. Joe saw her smile widen even more as she knelt to scratch Wishbone behind the ears.

"Well, what's your name, big fella?" she asked.

"His name is Wishbone," Joe explained. Then he added, "My name is Joe—Joe Talbot."

The lady rose to her feet and held out her right hand. "It's a pleasure to meet you, Joe. My name is Mrs. Millicent McKinley." She turned her attention back to Wishbone. "You're a fine-looking dog, Wishbone," Mrs. McKinley said. "I bet you would have liked my Tasha." She turned to Joe. "I used to have a black poodle named Tasha. She lived with me for a long, long time. Then she passed away about a year ago."

"I'm sorry," Joe replied.

"Don't be, Joe," Mrs. McKinley said. "She lived a

long, full life. In fact . . ." She trailed off as she turned to look at one of the card tables. She moved some porcelain figurines aside and picked up what looked like a small rubber cat. She knelt beside Wishbone. "I'm sure my Tasha would have loved for you to have this, Wishbone."

Wishbone's tail wagged as he gave the toy cat a sniff, then took it in his mouth. It let out a small squeak when he bit down on it, and his tail wagged faster.

"I think he likes it," Joe said. He then looked down at the box of baseball cards he was holding.

"Does five dollars sound like a reasonable price for the cards, Joe?" Mrs. McKinley asked.

"Yes, ma'am," Joe replied. He set the box on the corner of one of the card tables and began to search more carefully through the cards. Many of them were worth much more than that. But if the cards cost five dollars each, he could afford to buy only a couple of them.

"Mrs. McKinley, I like a lot of these cards, but I think I can only afford to buy a few."

"Joe," Mrs. McKinley told him, "I meant five dollars for the entire box."

Joe couldn't believe what he had just heard. His face lit up.

Mrs. McKinley quickly added, "And I'll even throw in the squeaky toy for free."

Joe dug into his pockets and pulled out a few singles and some change.

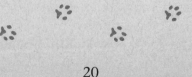

It's not often that I get to sink my teeth into a cat, Wishbone thought, as he lay on the living room floor chewing his new squeaky toy. Joe was sitting on the couch nearby. He had his father's baseball card album open on the coffee table, right next to the box of baseball cards he had bought from Mrs. McKinley.

Wishbone could hear Joe's mom, Ellen, in the kitchen, as she put away the dishes from dinner. And what a good dinner it had been. But, then again, Wishbone rarely met a dinner he didn't like.

Looking up at Joe between chews, Wishbone was happy that his pal was so excited about the cards he'd sniffed out for him. Wishbone had long ago learned to trust his nose.

Speaking of smells, it seemed that this squeaky cat didn't quite have the right odor yet. And the taste wasn't quite there, either. Wishbone got to his feet. *Not to worry,* Wishbone thought. *It isn't anything that a couple of days being buried in Wanda's yard won't cure.* Wishbone carried the toy through the living room and the kitchen, then exited the house by way of his doggie door.

Although it was dark and it would be difficult for anyone to spot him, Wishbone still was very careful as he made his way into his next-door neighbor's yard. He carefully crept into each shadow the streetlight had cast. Wishbone had to make sure Wanda didn't see him.

He and Wanda had a very special arrangement. Wishbone could bury all of his worldly possessions in her yard and flower beds anytime he wanted—as long as she didn't catch him doing it.

Wishbone crept slowly onto the side of Wanda's

porch and placed his front paws on her windowsill. Inside, he saw his auburn-haired neighbor bent over a large, flat spinning wheel with what looked like a large clump of mud sitting on top of it. The slender woman had both hands on either side of the clump. When she pressed inward, the mud began to get taller and taller.

"Interesting," Wishbone said. "I see I'm not the only one that likes to play with mud."

With Wanda occupied, the terrier hopped down from his perch and trotted off the porch and into her backyard. He set the toy down, sniffed the yard, circled once, then began to dig in a nice soft spot. It was time to make another deposit in the Wanda Gilmore Flower Bed Savings and Loan.

After just a few moments of having dirt fly between his back legs, Wishbone soon had a hole just the right size for the squeaky-toy-seasoning process. He picked up the rubber cat and dropped it into the newly dug hole.

"Chew you . . . I mean, *see you* in a couple of days, Mr. Cat!" Wishbone smiled as he quickly buried the toy with the dirt from the nearby pile.

When the hole was completely filled in, Wishbone began to look around the yard.

"Now," Wishbone said to himself, "where did I bury my squeaky book?" He gazed over to one of the darker parts of the yard. "Oh, right!"

Wishbone ran to a bush, ready to dig up his favorite toy that was buried behind it. When he reached the spot, however, he found that his squeaky-book hole had already been dug up.

"Oh, no!" he cried. "Someone took Squeaky!" He

looked at the edge of the hole, only to see his book resting safely inside the neatly dug opening. "Hey— you're *not* missing!"

It really wasn't like Wishbone to forget to cover up a hole. *Oh, well,* Wishbone thought, *even dogs sometimes make mistakes.* He stuck his muzzle into the hole and grabbed the toy between his teeth. It gave a satisfying sound when he did so. "Good evening, Mr. Squeaky," Wishbone said to his book. "I'll be your chewer this evening."

With the book in his mouth, Wishbone began to trot back to his house. As he went, a strange scent crossed in front of his nose. He stopped, set the book down, and raised his muzzle into the air. He caught one last whiff. Then the puzzling odor was gone. He turned in a circle and lifted his nose a bit higher as he sniffed again.

"Oh, well," Wishbone said as he picked up his book. "I'll just have to wait until later to identify that smell." He ran for the back door. "But now, it's chewing time!"

Joe smiled every time he pulled another card out of the box. Already he had been able to complete two of his dad's favorite teams, and start five more. And the shoe box was barely half empty! It seemed as if every card he turned over was like buried treasure.

Wishbone trotted into the living room, carrying his favorite rubber book. He wagged his tail as he plopped down on the middle of the floor and began to chew. Joe smiled at him, and Wishbone's tail seemed to wag even faster.

Joe returned his attention to the box of baseball cards. The next card he pulled out seemed to be one of the oldest ones yet. He carefully turned it over in his hand and, to his surprise, he saw the words "Oakdale Oaks" at the top of the card. The rest of the card showed a yellowing black-and-white photograph of a young black man. He held a baseball bat over his right shoulder as he posed for the photograph. According to the card, his name was Lindsay Groves. Upon turning the card over, Joe learned that Groves had been the relief pitcher for the Oakdale Oaks.

Joe couldn't believe it! He carefully set the card down and ran upstairs to his bedroom. On his bookshelf, he kept a photo album that doubled as a scrapbook. He grabbed the scrapbook and ran downstairs. He sat down on the couch and began to turn the pages of the book. Out of the corner of his eye, he saw Wishbone drop his toy and come to his side.

Joe turned another page of the scrapbook and came to what he was looking for. On one full page, under a clear-plastic protective cover, was the old baseball program Dr. Brown had given him.

About two years before, a woman named Dr. Thelma Brown came to Oakdale and visited Joe and his mom. As it turned out, her father had designed and built the house that he lived in now. Dr. Brown had spent most of her childhood growing up in their very house, and in Joe's very room. During her visit, she had told Joe about how she and her brother had buried a time capsule in the front yard many years ago.

After a little searching, and with the help of Wishbone's sharp nose for finding buried treasure, Joe, his mom, Sam, David, and Wanda Gilmore had found the old metal box that held small treasures from Dr. Brown's childhood. One of those treasures was a game program for the Oakdale Oaks, Oakdale's one and only Negro Baseball League team.

Now Joe had found an actual baseball card for one of its players—Lindsay Groves! Joe carefully examined the team photograph that was on the old program. Sure enough, in the second row, second to the end, was Lindsay Groves.

Joe returned his attention to the half-empty shoe box. Earlier, Joe had carefully pulled each card out of the box. He had either added it to one of his father's original teams, or added it to one of the new teams he had started from Mrs. McKinley's collection.

Now, he quickly removed the rest of the cards, one by one. He placed them neatly in stacks on the coffee table. Excited, he searched for any more Oaks cards he could find. Wishbone seemed to sense Joe's excitement, and he gave a small bark and wagged his tail.

After flipping through the cards, Joe didn't think he was going to find any more of what he was searching for. There were only a few cards left in the box. When he got to the last three, however, he found exactly what he was hoping to see. Another Oaks card—in fact, it was the team card! He held it up next to the team photo on the old program. He saw that the photographs on both were identical. Ten young black men dressed neatly in their team uniforms were standing, sitting, and kneeling for the shot. They were the Oaks, a professional baseball team from Oakdale.

Joe wasn't sure if he would be able to sleep tonight after his unexpected discovery. He was sure of one thing, though—he couldn't wait until tomorrow, when he would show David and Sam his great find.

Chapter Two

"Ah! It's great to be a dog," Wishbone said, as he took in a deep breath. "It's even better being a dog with a dog's special sense of smell!" The terrier breathed out. Then he took in another long breath through his nose— pepperonicheesehamburgerItaliansausagetomatoesonions-Canadianbaconpeppersmushrooms! "It's the greatest thing to be a dog with special smelling powers inside Pepper Pete's Pizza Parlor!"

Although the Monday lunch rush of business people was begining to slow down, the pizza parlor was still about half full of people talking and enjoying delicious pizza. The restaurant itself was decorated to look like a fine, casual Italian restaurant. Yet, the booths scattered around, the lively decor, plus the jukebox gave the place an informal atmosphere that attracted many kids, as well.

Wishbone was sitting on the floor next to the table where an enthusiastic Joe Talbot was sitting with his friend David. The terrier looked up to see David holding the two Oakdale Oaks cards that Joe had found the night before. Both of the cards were now in special clear-plastic protective sheets.

"I didn't even know the Negro Baseball League had baseball cards," David said excitedly. "I bet they're worth a fortune!"

Joe was looking at the old baseball program. It, too, was now in a clear-plastic sheet. "Probably, but I would never sell them," Joe replied. "I *am* interested in learning more about the team, though."

David nodded.

"Me, too," Sam said, as she walked by carrying a large pizza to a nearby booth. Wishbone knew she was trying hard to keep up with the boys' conversation while she was waiting on tables to help her dad.

"You know what I'd like, Sam?" Wishbone said. "One slice! That's what I'd like!" He sat up on his haunches and waved at the air with his front paws.

Sam didn't seem to notice. The dog sighed and turned back to watch Joe and David.

Joe continued his conversation. "Remember when Dr. Brown told us how she used to watch them play at Legion Field every Sunday afternoon?"

"It would have been great to see them play," David answered.

Out of the corner of Wishbone's eye, he watched Sam walk back to the kitchen with an empty tray. "It would've been *great* if at least one piece of pepperoni fell off." He took in another deep sniff of the restaurant's heavenly aroma. If he didn't get something to eat soon, all of the pizza smells teasing his nose were going to drive him crazy.

Sometimes I really don't like being a dog with a dog's exceptional sense of smell inside Pepper Pete's Pizza Parlor! he thought.

Sam came out of the kitchen with a tray of soft drinks for Joe and David. To Wishbone's delight, she brought a single bread stick, which she promptly gave to Wishbone. "Here you are, Wishbone," she said, as she handed him the bread stick.

Wishbone grabbed it thankfully and gobbled it up with pleasure. "You may not know it, Sam, but you just saved the day."

Joe watched as Wishbone swallowed the last crumbs of the bread stick. "The smell of pizza cooking sure can make you hungry, can't it, boy?"

Wishbone cocked his head, then gave a few small wags of his tail.

David was looking at Lindsay Groves's card. Joe held the Oakdale Oaks team card. Joe gazed at it and thought how cool it was to actually have a couple of baseball cards in his dad's collection that were from Oakdale itself. He wished his dad was still alive to see them. He then wondered if his dad had ever actually seen the Oaks play. Of course not, he realized. By the time his dad was born, there were no longer separate baseball leagues only for black players and white players.

Then, suddenly, Joe remembered someone whom he *knew* saw them play, and who also might be interested in seeing the baseball cards.

"You know, I bet Dr. Brown would be interested in seeing these cards," Joe said, turning the card over in his hand.

"Hey!" David agreed. "Great idea."

Sam cleared some empty plates off a neighboring table. "If you guys can wait about five minutes," she said, "I'll be done with my shift. We can all ride over together to visit her." Once more, she handed Wishbone a piece of a bread stick. The dog gobbled it up quickly.

"Sure," Joe replied. "I'll call Dr. Brown and let her know we are coming. But we'd better hurry before Wishbone eats Pepper Pete's out of business."

Everyone laughed, and Wishbone gave a couple of quick wags with his tail.

With Wishbone leading, Joe, Sam, and David rode their bikes across town to where Dr. Thelma Brown lived. Dr. Brown had moved away from Oakdale for many years during the time she actively practiced medicine. Then, after coming back to Oakdale for a visit after she retired, Dr. Brown decided to move into a small house there. She had bought a place just a few blocks from Joe's house. Joe was glad she did. She had told him and his friends some great stories about what Oakdale had been like years ago. If it hadn't been for her, Joe would never have heard of the Oakdale Oaks in the first place.

Joe watched as, once again, Wishbone kept a good enough distance between himself and the kids so he could investigate as much as possible. *He's always sniffing out something,* Joe thought, as Wishbone disappeared ahead of them.

The kids turned down Dr. Brown's street. They coasted down the small hill to the end, where her house was located. As they got closer, Joe saw that Dr. Brown was kneeling in the front yard working in one of her flower beds. The woman was dressed in denim overalls that were spotted with small smudges of dirt. Bits of her curly, gray hair were sticking out from under her straw sun hat. With one gloved hand, she was petting a very familiar white dog with brown and black spots.

Joe, Sam, and David parked their bikes on the sidewalk. Then they walked over to Dr. Brown and Wishbone.

"Hi, kids," Dr. Brown said, waving a gloved hand. Everyone greeted her as they made their way across the yard.

"We've got something great to show you, Dr. Brown!" Joe announced excitedly.

The doctor gave Wishbone one more scratch behind the ears. Then she slowly got to her feet. She removed her gardening gloves and met the kids halfway across her lawn.

Joe, Sam, and David met Dr. Brown underneath the shade of a large pecan tree. Joe slung his backpack off his shoulder and unzipped the main pocket. He reached in and took out the two baseball cards and handed them to Dr. Brown. He also pulled out the old Oakdale Oaks program.

Dr. Brown took the cards in her hand and looked them over. She paused for a moment, then smiled.

"Why, I haven't seen any of these in more than sixty years," she remarked with delight. She pointed a finger to the team card. "In fact, I used to have one of these team cards myself."

Joe, David, and Sam looked at one another and smiled. Then Joe looked back at Dr. Brown. By the expression on her face, he could tell she was deep in distant memories.

"Where did you ever get these, Joe?" she asked, still looking at the old cards.

Joe explained about how Wishbone had found the cards at the yard sale as they were returning from playing ball at Legion Field.

"These are quite a find," Dr. Brown commented.

Wishbone gave a little bark and raised a front paw into the air.

Dr. Brown bent over and gave the terrier a pat on the head. "Good job, Wishbone," she told him.

"You saw the Oaks play, didn't you, Dr. Brown?" David asked.

"Many times, David, many times," the doctor replied, standing up.

"Do you remember Lindsay Groves?" Sam asked Dr. Brown.

"Oh, Samantha," Dr. Brown said, as she looked at the Lindsay Groves card. "It's been so long ago. I can't say that I do."

"I hope you don't mind all the questions, Dr. Brown," Joe said. "We're just really interested in learning more about the Oaks."

"That's quite all right, Joe," Dr. Brown replied. "You should be interested. They're part of this town's history."

"I wish I could have seen them play," Joe said.

Dr. Brown took off her sun hat and wiped her brow with the back of one hand. "I tell you, Joe," she said, "it was something. When I was only eight or nine years old, my parents used to take my little brother and me over to Legion Field every Sunday afternoon. We were all dressed in our finest clothes, which we had worn to church earlier that morning. Most everyone went to the field dressed in their Sunday best."

She placed her hat back on her head and passed the cards to Joe.

The reason the Oakdale Oaks and the Negro Baseball League were formed was because the professional baseball leagues at that time didn't allow black people to play on their teams.

"You kids are lucky," Dr. Brown continued. "You live in a more accepting time, and in a town where the color of a person's skin isn't an issue." Dr. Brown slowly walked back to her flower bed. Wishbone and the kids followed her.

"That doesn't seem fair," Sam said, with sadness in her voice.

"It wasn't," Dr. Brown responded, "especially when the Negro League players were just as talented as anyone else who played the game."

Joe noticed that Wishbone was lightly nuzzling Dr. Brown's pants leg.

She knelt down and gave him a scratch on top of his head. "In fact, if I remember correctly, the Oakdale Oaks won the national championship one year."

"The *championship*?" Joe asked excitedly.

"I'm almost sure of it," Dr. Brown said. "I remember my parents being very excited about it."

"Wow! A championship team from Oakdale," Sam said, looking gleefully at Joe and David.

Joe looked down at the cards. They didn't mention anything about a championship. Of course, they could have been printed before the Oaks had won it.

Joe turned to Sam and David. "Do you two want to go to the library with me and find out if these were the actual players who won the championship?"

Both David and Sam gave their agreement. The kids said good-bye to Dr. Brown and started to bicycle back toward the center of town. Joe turned around and watched as Wishbone managed to get one more ear scratch out of the retired doctor. Then the dog took off behind the three kids.

Chapter Three

Joe pulled open the front door of the Henderson Memorial Library and stepped into a wall of cool, air-conditioned air. All around him, he smelled the familiar, pleasant odor of old books. Sam and David entered the library behind him. Joe looked back, just in time, to see Wishbone slowly enter. It seemed he still wasn't completely comfortable going inside. Up until recently, Wishbone had not been allowed into the library. Joe couldn't understand why. After all, Wishbone was very well behaved. Besides, no one seemed to mind. And, of course, Joe's mom was the head librarian.

"It's okay, boy," Joe said. "Just remember to be on your best behavior." Wishbone gave two quick wags of his tail. Then he raised his nose into the air to sniff. Joe understood that he wasn't the only one who liked the smell of old books.

The kids turned right inside the library's foyer. They approached the front counter, directly in front of them. To the left of the front counter, Joe saw the multimedia area where the computers, microfiche machines, and magazines were stationed. Across the library, he saw his mom come out from between a row of shelves. Ellen Talbot was carrying a large stack of books. They were piled almost as high as the slender woman's head. Her short, brown hair seemed a bit tousled as she carried the stack to the middle of the library and set it onto one of the tables there.

A number of opened books were scattered on the table. Sitting there studying them was a thin man who appeared to be in his early forties. He wore jeans and a brown sportcoat. The man had short, brown curly hair and wore reading glasses. He was concentrating hard on the book he was reading at the moment. When Ellen set the books down, he thanked her and said he hoped he was not troubling her too much. She replied, "It was no trouble, Mr. Carroll."

Then the man returned to his reading. Joe thought the guy looked just like he did when he was studying for an exam at school.

Ellen walked back to the front counter, rubbing her right shoulder as she went. "Hi, kids," she said, greeting them. Then she looked down at Wishbone. "Hi, Wishbone." He wagged his tail. Joe was proud that the dog knew better than to bark.

"I'm really busy today," Ellen said with a smile, still rubbing her shoulder. "What are you up to?"

"We came to do a little research," Joe explained. "We'd like to find out more about the Oakdale Oaks."

"That's right—your new baseball cards," Ellen said with a smile. "Where would you like to start?"

Joe explained how they had visited Dr. Brown, and how she told them about the Oaks winning the championship.

"Well, Joe," Ellen said, "if any Oakdale team won a *national* championship, I'm sure there had to have been an article written about it in *The Oakdale Chronicle*. What year should we start in?"

Joe pulled out the team card again from his backpack. "It says this was the 1932 team," Joe told his mom. "Let's check April through September—baseball season."

David added, "Or we could start with March 1932. Maybe we'd catch something about spring training."

"March through September of 1932 it is," Ellen said.

She left the kids and entered the main office. When she returned, she had a few small folders, no bigger than postcards, in her hand. "Here's the first few months' worth of *Chronicle* issues on microfiche," she said. She motioned to the multimedia area of the library.

The kids followed Ellen as she led the way. Wishbone wove between them. He jumped onto a chair in front of the microfiche viewer.

"Thanks, Wishbone, but I think I'd better handle this," Sam said jokingly.

Wishbone hopped down and Sam took his place.

Ellen handed her a small folder. Sam removed the first sheet of microfiche, which was just a thin piece of plastic. Joe could see the tiny pages of newspaper that were printed on it.

Sam pulled a lever sticking out from under the large screen. Two horizontal pieces of glass opened up like a transparent clam. Then she placed the microfiche in between the glass and pushed the lever back. The two pieces of glass closed over the microfiche and retreated into the machine. With a flick of the power switch, the screen lit up with a page from the newspaper.

Joe watched as Sam moved the lever back and forth, scanning for any mention of the team and the championship. Luckily, there was more than one issue of the *Chronicle* on each sheet of microfiche, so the kids were able to search quickly.

Joe watched as pictures, words, and headlines from another time in history crossed the screen in a slight blur. The kids searched several sheets, scanning each issue, especially the sports section. They didn't find anything mentioned about the championship, or even about the Oakdale Oaks themselves.

"This is really weird," Sam said as she continued to move the lever. "There's nothing in these issues about the Oaks at all." She pulled out the microfiche and replaced it with another one. "You think there would be at least game scores or something."

"Here's another few months' worth," Ellen said. She handed Joe the small protective sleeves. "I have to help someone else, but I'll be back in a moment." Ellen returned to the front counter as Sam placed the next microfiche in the viewer.

Sitting at Joe's feet, Wishbone reared up onto his haunches and looked longingly toward the machine. To Joe, it seemed as if Wishbone wanted to play with the microfiche viewer.

Page after page slowly went by. Then something finally caught Joe's eye. "Wait a minute, Sam," he said eagerly. "Go back."

Sam stopped and slowly moved the image in the opposite direction.

"There," Joe said immediately. "Just at the end of the sports section."

Sam stopped flipping. Everyone leaned in as Joe pointed to a small box near the bottom of the page. In the box was a list of several scores of different baseball games. At the end there was a final score that read: Oakdale Oaks: 15; Whitenfield Kings: 7.

There it was. It wasn't much, but it was something concrete. Other than Joe's two newly discovered baseball cards and the old team program, this was the first evidence the kids had found that the Oaks even existed.

"What's the date of this issue?" Joe asked.

Sam scrolled the image down until the top of the paper was visible. Sam read it aloud: "May 22, 1932."

"May 22?" Joe asked, unbelieving.

"Yes," Sam replied. "Is something wrong?"

Joe leaned in a little closer. "Could you go back to the front page for a minute?" Sam adjusted the lever, and the newsprint whizzed by. She stopped when she reached the front page. "Does any of this look familiar to you, Sam?"

"Does what look familiar?" David asked.

Sam's eyes widened. "Yes!" She scrolled up to the top of the page.

Joe pointed to the top of the front page. Then he and Sam said at the same time, "Owned and operated by Giles Gilmore." Joe and Sam each gave a small laugh.

"So what's so funny about that?" David asked.

"Joe and I have seen this issue before!" Sam said, spinning around in her seat to face David.

"Remember when your family got back from vacation and we told you about how that news reporter had spread all those nasty rumors about Miss Gilmore?" Joe asked.

"And how the reporter said Miss Gilmore didn't rightfully own *The Oakdale Chronicle*?" Sam asked.

"Yes. You said she almost lost the newspaper to Mr. King," David replied. "But what does that have to do with the Oakdale Oaks?"

Sam took over. "When Joe and I were looking for clues about how Miss Gilmore's father, Giles Gilmore, actually came to own the *Chronicle,* we came across this issue." She looked over her shoulder to the screen. "I thought it seemed familiar," she said to herself. Then she turned back to David. "We found out that Giles Gilmore actually won the *Chronicle* from its previous owner, Abel Skelton, in a poker game on the night of May 21, 1932."

"And," Joe continued, "this is the first issue to mention the Oaks. This is also the very first issue of the paper that was printed by Wanda's father."

"So," David asked, "what does it all mean?"

Joe couldn't help smiling. "I *bet* it means that Abel Skelton wasn't a very big Oaks fan."

Wishbone reared up on his haunches for what seemed like the fifieth time. "Saaaaaam," he whined. "It's my turn to play with the viewer!" He pawed the air, trying his best not to bark. He loved to place his paw on the machine's positioning knob and move the image of the newspaper around the screen. "Come on, Sam! You know, paper goes up, paper goes down!" Wishbone finally gave up and sat back down. It seemed as if no one ever listened to the dog.

No one was really going to listen to him now. Joe, Sam, and David were too excited. Wishbone watched as Ellen came over with a fresh batch of newspaper issues.

"Have you found anything yet?" she asked. She set down the next batch of newspaper microfiche.

"We sure have!" Joe answered with excitement in his voice. Wishbone thought if Joe had a tail right now, he'd be wagging it pretty hard.

Sam reloaded the viewer with one of the issues Ellen had just brought over. "After Giles Gilmore took over the *Chronicle,* the paper started to print articles about the Oakdale Oaks," she told Ellen.

"Yes," David agreed. "We've found articles about the team's origin, player biographies, and even accounts of the games!"

"We still haven't found anything about the championship, though," Joe said. "After we do, I want to come back and read some of these articles thoroughly."

Wishbone was about to make one final plea for a turn at the microfiche viewer. Suddenly, out of the corner of his eye, he saw a large shadow behind them. With extremely fast doglike reflexes, Wishbone stood and spun around, ready to defend his group. To his surprise, it was only Mr. Carroll.

He was edging along a nearby magazine rack, his fingers running over some of the covers. When Wishbone jumped up, Mr. Carroll's eyes shifted to the terrier. Then his glance quickly turned to some books nearby.

"Fear not, citizens," Wishbone announced. "I just switched into guard-dog mode for a moment." Wishbone sat back down. "But don't worry, I'm at ease now."

Wishbone stood, circled once, then lay down beside Sam's chair. *Now he's looking for magazines?* Wishbone thought. *Mr. Carroll would have to be some kind of fast reader to have looked over all the books Ellen already brought him.*

Wishbone wondered if Mr. Carroll had a problem with having a dog in the library. He decided to lie low. Ellen had just started to allow him to come inside. He didn't want to lose his library privileges.

"Things are starting to slow down," Sam said as she scanned the next issue in the viewer. "After the 1932 baseball season ended, the Oaks traveled around and played a few exhibition games, but that seems to be about it for the year."

Joe turned to his mom. "Could we see the next year?" he asked.

"Sure," Ellen replied, turning and heading for the office. "Just a moment—1933 coming up!"

As Ellen walked around the corner, Sam got out of her seat and stretched her legs. "I wonder how many years the Oaks were together," she said.

Wishbone saw his chance! He hopped onto the chair and faced the microfiche viewer. This was going to be great!

"Well," David replied, "there aren't any Negro leagues today, so the team must have disbanded quite some time ago."

Wishbone put his paw on the little lever and began to move it back and forth. "Newspaper goes up! Newpaper goes down!"

"I don't believe it!" Ellen said all of a sudden, as she walked back toward the kids.

Startled, Wishbone turned around to see Ellen quickly enter the microfiche room. "I'm sorry, Ellen," Wishbone said as he hopped out of the chair. "I was just looking for some dog-food coupons—you know, trying to help you out."

"What's wrong?" Joe asked his mom.

"The year 1933," Ellen said, "it's gone!"

"What?" David asked in disbelief.

"I mean, the whole year is gone!" Ellen said. "An entire year of Oakdale's history is missing!"

Chapter Four

"Ah, the Oakdale *Chronicle* archives," Wishbone said. He followed Joe, David, Sam, and Wanda Gilmore down the *Chronicle*'s basement steps. Since Wishbone's last visit to the *Chronicle,* Wanda had moved all her archives to the basement. He couldn't wait to get down there and start sniffing around.

"I can't believe the whole year of 1933 is missing from the library's microfiche files," Wanda said as she flicked the light switch at the bottom of the steps. "Do you think it was just misplaced?"

Wishbone watched from the middle of the staircase as a soft, pale-green glow from the fluorescent lights flickered on below him.

"That's what my mom's looking into right now," Joe answered.

"Well, if the year doesn't turn up," Wanda stated, "she's welcome to borrow the *Chronicle*'s hard copies and make another set of microfiches."

"I'm sure she'd appreciate that," Joe replied.

"After all," Wanda continued, "people need to have access to the rich and wonderful history of Oakdale!"

Wishbone hopped off the last step and looked around the *Chronicle*'s basement archives. The basement was quite large, running under the entire *Chronicle* building. It was also very quiet. Too quiet.

Wishbone looked around and saw the rows and rows of shelves, each filled with identical white cardboard boxes. Wishbone assumed that was where the back issues of the newspaper were kept. The place was lit by only a few rows of fluorescent lights near the middle of the room, so long shadows that were cast by the shelves crept toward the walls. Wishbone could make out old signs and banners leaning against the back wall. He also noticed some filing cabinets, odds and ends, and what appeared to be an old-fashioned printing press.

"Okay, nose," Wishbone said to himself, "time to get sniffing!" Wishbone broke off from the group and headed for all the interesting materials stacked against the walls. White boxes of old newspapers all smelled alike. The really good aromas were going to be with the other items. He did, however, keep an ear open to Wanda and the kids, just in case they needed him.

"Okay," Wanda began, "what year were you looking for?"

"The year 1933," David replied quickly.

Wishbone turned and saw Wanda begin to scan the shelves. He turned back to sniff at the base of an old Oakdale Historical Society sign. The sign was resting upside down, against the basement wall. The tip of its stake was crusted with dirt. "Hmm," Wishbone said to himself, "it smells as if this was posted in Jackson Park. It also smells as if I'm not the first dog to investigate it."

"Oh, my!" Wanda said from across the room.

The terrier turned and trotted over to see what was wrong.

"What's wrong, Miss Gilmore?" Sam asked.

"It's not here," Wanda answered, unbelieving. "The boxes go directly from 1932 to 1934—nothing in between!" She put a finger on the label of a white box. Then she pointed to another box.

"You're missing that same year, too?" Joe asked in disbelief.

"Maybe the boxes containing 1933 are just out of sequence," Wanda said hopefully. She turned to the group. "Kids, we need to check every box!"

Everyone split up and began to examine the labels on each box. Wishbone stayed with Joe. He could sense his friend's frustration, and he was ready to offer a little canine moral support if it was needed.

With four of them looking, it didn't take long to read every label in the place. Unfortunately, the boxes containing the 1933 archives were still missing.

"This is a dark day for Oakdale," Wanda said dramatically. "As the president of the Oakdale Historical Society, I declare this to be a town disaster!"

First the microfiche, and now all the hard copies? This can't be just a coincidence, Joe thought.

"Why would anyone want to steal a year's worth of newspapers?" David asked. Obviously, he didn't think the missing newspapers was a coincidence, either.

"Not only *why*," Sam added, "but *who?*"

Wanda had begun to scan the boxes again. "I don't know, Sam," she said, as she disappeared behind a shelf. The kids followed her around. "I don't see how anyone could have taken all the boxes out of here without someone noticing." Suddenly, Wanda stopped and placed her hands on both sides of her face. "What if they've been kidnapped!" Wanda held both hands out in front of her and then spread them in the air, as if she were laying down a headline. "Oakdale's history held for ransom!" she said.

"I wonder if it has anything to do with the Oaks," David said curiously.

"The Oaks?" Wanda asked.

"Yes," Joe said. He walked over to the foot of the basement steps and picked up his backpack. He opened the main compartment and, once again, took out the two baseball cards. Joe walked back and handed them to Wanda. "This is why we were looking for the year 1933 in the first place."

Wanda's eyes widened as she gazed at the two cards. "I haven't seen one of these cards in years," she said in amazement. "In fact, my father used to have the entire set."

"Your father collected the Oaks baseball cards?" Joe asked. His excitement over the cards was building again.

"Collected them?" Wanda questioned. She then turned the Lindsay Groves card over and pointed to a very tiny line of type in one corner. Joe leaned in to get a closer look. He was surprised to find out the logo was that of *The Oakdale Chronicle*. "Joe," Wanda continued, "my father *printed* the Oaks baseball cards."

"It makes perfect sense," said David, "especially after we found all of the Oakdale Oaks articles in the paper after Mr. Gilmore took over the *Chronicle*."

"That's right, David," Wanda explained. "My father was a very big supporter of the Oaks. In fact, baseball cards for the Negro League teams were almost nonexistent." She turned the team card over in her hand. "My father decided to print these up himself." Wanda handed the cards back to Joe. "They're very rare, Joe, and most likely very valuable."

Joe took the cards and placed them into his backpack with even more care than before.

"I'd be more than happy to help you research the team, Joe," Wanda said, as she returned to the rows of white boxes. "But first I have to find out what happened to the missing year."

Once again the kids split up and helped Wanda scan the labels on the boxes. Joe was sure they hadn't overlooked the missing 1933 boxes on their first search. He was almost positive that the missing year had something to do with the Oakdale Oaks.

Chapter Five

Joe sat back in his bed and stared, daydreaming, into the darkness outside his bedroom window. Beside him on the floor was Wishbone, slowly chewing his book-shaped squeaky toy.

The light from the lamp on Joe's nightstand shined over the two baseball cards in his hand. Slowly and carefully he took each card out of its protective sleeve and moved his fingers over them. Sometimes things felt more real when they could actually be touched. And Joe wanted to touch them now, because he had come to a difficult and unpleasant decision. The next day, he planned to return these two cards to Mrs. McKinley. It was a difficult choice to make, but it was the right one. Joe was sure Mrs. McKinley had no idea how important the cards were when she had sold them to him.

They were far too valuable to be passed off in a box full of other cards in a yard sale.

Joe took one more look at the cards. Then he

placed them on his nightstand and closed his eyes. In his imagination, he began to hear a low murmur. Slowly the murmur became louder. It grew until it became the sound of a large stadium full of people cheering. Joe could feel warm sunlight slowly heating the skin on his arms and the back of his neck.

Then he felt a cool breeze that ruffled his short hair. The breeze itself carried a variety of scents, from hot dogs and roasted peanuts to the various smells of a large group of people's mixed colognes and perfumes. On either side of him, he felt the presence of people around him.

Joe pictured himself inside Legion Field—sitting in the bleachers. And this was not the Legion Field he knew. This was the Legion Field of 1933. The bleachers were no longer warped planks of painted, chipped wood. Instead, they looked new and were painted a bright, deep blue. The field itself was covered with rich, short green grass, not a combination of weeds, grass, and dirt. Instead of being covered with old, faded lettering, the black wall was plastered with proud advertisements for different local businesses.

Joe looked down onto the field to find it occupied by the proud Oakdale Oaks. Their clean, baggy uniforms billowed in the wind. The word "Oakdale" was written across each of their chests in bold maroon letters.

Joe heard a crack at the plate. He watched as one of the opposing team's players hit a fly ball over center field. The batter never had a chance to make it to first base. An Oaks outfielder easily caught the ball, then drilled it to the second baseman, who then picked off the player heading for second base. A perfect double play!

Joe's attention came back quickly to the bleachers as a deafening roar rose from the people around him. He looked around and saw hundreds of well-dressed black people of all ages having what seemed to be the best time of their lives.

People were cheering, patting each other on the back, pointing to the field with wide smiles on their faces. Soon everyone sat down and watched with anticipation for the next play. They ate hot dogs and peanuts.

Then Joe made an interesting discovery. It occurred to him, as he looked around at the crowd, that he was the only white person there. Suddenly, Joe's daydream took an uncomfortable turn. One by

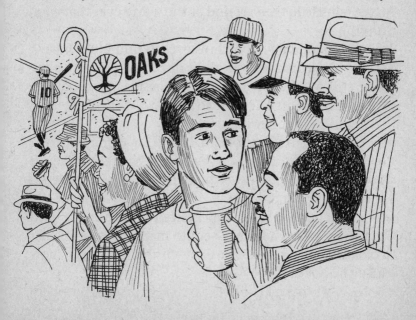

one, the other spectators turned to him and stared. The crowd slowly took its attention away from the field and aimed it at the fourteen-year-old boy who was sitting with them in the bleachers—the fourteen-year-old *white* boy. Joe's discomfort grew as the cheering died down and the breeze stopped blowing. In his dream, everyone now faced him—staring in silence. Even the two teams below had temporarily stopped their game to watch Joe Talbot, the white boy, as he sat in the stands.

Did they mind him being there? Did they want him to leave because of the color of his skin? Maybe they would rather have him go and watch his own baseball league—the white league—the league their own players weren't allowed to join. Then it occurred to Joe—that was how the Negro League players must have felt. He looked around at the many eyes that were on him.

Joe suddenly opened his eyes to find himself back inside his bedroom in modern-day Oakdale. Wishbone was still playing with his toy beside the bed. He wagged his short tail as he looked at Joe. Then the dog returned to his chewing project.

Joe took in a deep breath, held it for a moment, then breathed out. It felt good to be back in the comfort of his own room. Joe had never had any personal experience with racial prejudice before. He had learned about the idea of it, but had never experienced the reality. He lived in a town where it didn't seem to matter to people what color someone else's skin was. He thought about how lucky he was to live in Oakdale.

Joe picked up the two baseball cards and put them

back into their protective sleeves. He placed them on his bedside table, next to the book he was reading. It was called *The Return of Sherlock Holmes,* by Sir Arthur Conan Doyle. The book was a collection of short stories that had been previously published in a British magazine called *The Strand* in 1904. Joe was halfway finished reading the book.

As he saw the volume, Joe's mind went back to his own mystery—the one of the missing newspapers. Why would anyone want to steal an entire year of Oakdale's history? Joe lay back and placed his hands behind his head. No answer came. It was as if he kept hitting a mental brick wall.

Joe's thoughts crept to one of the short stories. In one particular story, Sherlock Holmes felt almost the same way Joe did right now. The story was called "The Adventure of the Norwood Builder." In it, Sherlock Holmes was asked by a young lawyer, named John McFarlane, to help save him from being accused of a murder. Mr. McFarlane was charged with murdering one of his own clients, Jonas Oldacre, and burning the body.

Holmes thoroughly investigated the case. Unfortunately, every bit of evidence seemed to point to his client, Mr. McFarlane. Mr. McFarlane was the last person seen with Mr. Oldacre. Mr. McFarlane's cane, which was covered with blood, was found in Mr. Oldacre's study. The study itself held signs of a murderous struggle. To top it all off, there were clues that something very large had been dragged to Mr. Oldacre's neighboring lumber yard and had been burned on top of a large pile of wood. The situation looked bad for Mr. McFarlane. Yet Holmes believed there was more to the case than met the eye.

Joe's attention moved from the book to the cards sitting beside it. As Lindsay Groves and the 1932 Oakdale Oaks team stared back at him, Joe felt there was one thing he could be sure about—returning the cards to Mrs. McKinley was the right thing to do.

As Wishbone chewed on his squeaky book with great concentration, he sensed that Joe had suddenly felt a bit uneasy. The canine clamped down on his book, stood, then placed his front paws on the edge of Joe's bed.

"Here, Joe," Wishbone said. He placed the toy on the edge of the bed. "A good chew always makes me feel better!" With the tip of his nose, Wishbone nudged the book toward his best friend.

Joe picked up the toy and handed it back to Wishbone. "None for me, Wishbone," he said, joking. "It's time to go to bed." Joe rolled over and turned out the lamp on his nightstand. "We have to ride across town and see Mrs. McKinley tomorrow." With the moonlight that shone through the window, Wishbone saw Joe grab his pillow, roll over, and get ready to go to sleep. "Good night, Wishbone."

Wishbone grabbed his favorite toy. "Good night, Joe," he said.

The little dog hopped down and prepared for a few more chews before bedtime.

"Wait a minute," Wishbone said. "That reminds

me!" He dropped the book, ran out of Joe's room, and trotted down the stairs, toward the kitchen.

Until just then, Wishbone had forgotten all about the new rubber cat Mrs. McKinley had given him. He figured now was sure to be a good time to check to see if the toy was properly seasoned.

The terrier pushed through his doggie door and ran into the backyard. He hopped over a small hedge that was on the border of the Gilmore and Talbot property. Then, when his paws hit Wanda's yard, Wishbone immediately changed into Stealth Dog.

"Stealth Dog carefully maneuvering in," he said to himself in a deep voice as he crept slowly from shadow to shadow. He didn't want to run into Wanda. After what had happened that day at the *Chronicle*, she would not be in a good mood.

Looking over his shoulder, Wishbone slowly crawled over to the spot where he had buried the rubber cat. Unfortunately, since he wasn't watching where he was going, Wishbone fell, headfirst, into a freshly dug hole.

"Whoooooooooaaaa!"

Wishbone's front paws and the front half his body were now at the bottom of the shallow hole.

"Hey!?" Wishbone said in alarm.

The dog gradually backed out of the hole and shook some dirt out of his fur. He looked into the dark hole and with his sharp vision could see Mrs. McKinley's gift, sitting at the bottom.

Forgetting to cover one hole might have been just a mistake, but no dog worth half his fur would ever

forget to cover *two* holes! There was something definitely wrong with this picture!

Forgetting about being Stealth Dog for a moment, Wishbone trotted around the rest of Wanda's backyard and flower beds only to find five more open holes. "I may have to start looking for a better savings bank," he said. He began to refill the holes. "It seems that I am not this yard's only customer."

When Wishbone came upon the last open hole, he looked inside and found it empty. His mind raced, trying to remember what he had stashed there. The terrier carefully inched his way down to catch a whiff of whatever had been buried. He pressed his nose against the cool dirt and took in a shallow breath.

"T-bone!" Wishbone yelled, as he leaped out of the hole and looked all around. Someone had stolen the leftover T-bone Ellen had given him three weeks ago! Checking out his treasures was one thing, but now someone was stealing his possessions!

Wishbone placed his nose to the ground and began to sniff all around the open hole. Whoever had taken his delicious treasure was bound to have left a trail! He searched and searched, but all he found was that *new* smell. It was the smell he didn't have a name for yet. He knew it only as the stale, musky, new smell. It seemed to be much stronger now than it had been the first time he smelled it in Wanda's yard.

Could the odor be related to the theft of his bone? Once, Wishbone came across a gopher digging around in Wanda's flower garden. He smelled the ground again, then compared the scent to the cataloged gopher scent in his memory. *Nope,* he thought, *not the gopher smell.* Besides, the gopher's main attack had come from tunnels below the ground. Whoever this was, he or she was digging holes the old-fashioned way—from the top.

One thing is for sure, Wishbone thought. *It seems that newspapers aren't the only things ending up missing in Oakdale!*

Chapter Six

"Come in, Joe," Mrs. McKinley said, as she swung open her screen door. "I wasn't expecting to see you again so soon." Joe watched as she bent over and rubbed a hand across Wishbone's head. "It's good to see you, too, Wishbone." He gave a few quick wags of his tail, then accepted her invitation.

"I hope we're not disturbing you this morning, Mrs. McKinley," Joe said politely.

"Not at all, Joe," she replied, as she ushered him to a chair in her living room. Wishbone began to sniff all around the well-kept living room. After Joe sat down, Mrs. McKinley asked, "So, what brings you here?"

This was it. Joe hesitated slightly, then reached into his shirt pocket to remove the two sealed baseball cards. "I found these among the other cards you sold me," he said as he handed her the Oaks cards.

Mrs. McKinley took them in one hand. With her other hand, she reached for a pair of reading glasses on the coffee table. She put them on, then examined the cards.

Joe continued. "As you can see, they're from the Negro League. You may not know it, but there were hardly any baseball cards printed for the Negro League." He cleared his throat after noticing it had suddenly become very dry. "So these cards are probably very valuable. I couldn't let you sell them to me for five dollars."

Mrs. McKinley continued to examine the cards in silence. Finally, she spoke. "You're probably right, Joe," she said, as she took off her glasses. "I bet these could be worth a fortune." She looked at the cards once more, then held them out to Joe. "I'm sure they'll be a fine addition to your father's collection."

Joe couldn't believe his ears. "But—" he started to say.

"There are no 'buts' about it," she interrupted, holding up the cards. "Do you know why I sold all those cards to you so cheap?" she asked.

Speechless, Joe just shook his head.

"You see, Joe," Mrs. McKinley said, "all of those cards belonged to my late husband, Richard. That was his collection." She casually leaned back against the couch. "Now, mind you, he didn't keep them in protective plastic the way you've done." She held up the cards. "And he didn't even use folders or notebooks. But he was proud of his cards, just the same. In fact, some of them, like these here, he got when he was quite young."

Joe felt warm fur against the inside of his hand. He turned to see that Wishbone had nudged his hand that was hanging off of the sofa's arm rest.

"You see, Joe," Mrs. McKinley continued, "like you, Richard loved baseball. Those cards represented little pieces of the game he could keep for himself. He collected the cards of his favorite teams or of his favorite players. He collected them simply for *his* pleasure. He never cared whether the cards had any great money value." She leaned forward and spoke in a lower tone. "So, Joe, when you told me about how you were adding to your father's collection, I couldn't think of a more suitable home for Richard's cards."

Joe smiled as he took the two cards from her hands. "Thank you, Mrs. McKinley," he said, with a small lump in his throat.

With the matter of the baseball cards settled, Wishbone carefully gave Mrs. McKinley's place a sniff-over. Above him, Joe was telling the woman the story of the missing year's worth of newspapers.

"The entire year?" Mrs. McKinley asked.

"The entire set of microfiches *and* all of the hard copies from the *Chronicle*'s archives," Joe emphasized.

While Joe finished telling Mrs. McKinley about the mysterious disappearance, Wishbone continued to sniff around the living room. As he did, his nose identified faint traces of Tasha, the little black poodle. In his mind, Wishbone pictured Tasha lying on the living room rug, chewing the rubber cat that Mrs. McKinley had now given to him. He thought Tasha would be happy to know that the little cat was going to get worked over plenty.

Wishbone turned an ear toward Joe and Mrs. McKinley. Joe had just finished telling her about how he, Sam, and David suspected the Oakdale Oaks might have something to do with the disappearance of the year's newspapers.

"You know, Joe," Mrs. McKinley said, "I don't remember anything about them winning the championship. I do remember, though, reading about them somewhere other than in the newspaper." Joe leaned forward eagerly as Mrs. McKinley scrunched up her face, trying to remember. "If I recall correctly," she continued, "there was a locally published book about the history of Oakdale."

She stood and walked over to a small bookshelf in one corner of the living room. After giving it a quick scan, she turned back to Joe.

"I don't suppose I have it anymore," she said. She made her way back to the couch. "It *has* been a very long time since I've read it." She sat down. "I wish I could remember the name. It was green and it had a picture of a giant oak tree on the cover."

From the expression on Joe's face, Wishbone could see that a lightbulb had lit up in his head. "I remember that book!" Joe said excitedly. "I checked it out of the library last year for a social studies report! I can't believe I didn't think of it before!"

"Well, there you have it, Joe," Mrs. McKinley said. "Maybe the answers you are looking for are in that book."

"Thank you, Mrs. McKinley," he said, as he rose from his seat. Hearing Joe's farewell tone, Wishbone walked over to his side. Mrs. McKinley stood and walked them to the front door. "I'm really grateful for your help," Joe said. "And I really appreciate the baseball cards."

"Think nothing of it, Joe," she replied. "Just enjoy them."

The bright morning sun shone on Joe and Wishbone as they stepped out into Mrs. McKinley's front yard. "Don't worry, Mrs. McKinley," Joe answered, "I will." Joe walked down the sidewalk and got on his bicycle.

Wishbone didn't wait. He took off down the sidewalk, putting a little distance between himself and Joe. Even though they were just in this neighborhood two days ago, Wishbone wanted to sniff out as much as he could. After all, a lot could happen in two days.

The tones chimed in David's ear as he dialed the last four digits of the phone number: 7-6-0-4. He was standing in his family's kitchen beside the counter that separated the main part of the kitchen from the small breakfast area on the opposite side. He looked over at Sam, who was sitting at the small table in that area. Spread out before her were various books that included information about the Negro League. He and Sam had just checked them out of the library.

David looked down to the computer printout in his hand. On it were four names and phone numbers—the names and numbers of four living relatives of the Oakdale Oaks.

Earlier, David had done a quick search on the Internet for clues about the missing year. He hadn't run across the names of any of the original players themselves. But, after all, he hadn't done an in-depth search. He was sure he would come across more names later, when he had more time.

David felt a bit nervous making the calls. But he told himself that the relatives of the Oaks would be happy to talk to someone who was interested in their family history.

There was a click and a woman's voice answered. "Hello?"

David cleared his throat and spoke into the mouthpiece. "Hello. May I speak with Mrs. Denise Johnson?"

"Speaking," the voice replied quickly.

"Mrs. Johnson," David began, "my name is David Barnes. I'm calling from Oakdale, where I understand your grandfather—"

David didn't even get to finish. "Oakdale?" Mrs. Johnson interrupted in a harsh tone. "I'm not talking to anyone from Oakdale!" There was a sudden click as she hung up the phone.

"What's wrong?" Sam asked.

David thought his expression must have been revealing the surprise he felt. "She hung up on me," he replied, confused.

"What?" Sam asked, as if she couldn't believe it. "Why?"

"I have no idea," David answered. "She said she wouldn't talk to anyone who lived in Oakdale." He looked down at the list in his hand. He still felt a bit shocked.

"There must have been some kind of misunderstanding," Sam said, sounding as if she was trying to make sense of it all. "Why don't you call her back and find out?"

"I don't know. . . ." David picked up the wall phone once more. "Let me try another number."

The next two calls David made went just like the first one. The person on the other end of the phone line was very polite until David mentioned where he was from.

"What's going on?" Sam said after David had made his third call.

"I'm going to try another approach," David said. He dialed the last number on the page. The phone clicked in David's ear. Then it began to ring, once . . . twice . . . three times. . . .

There was a louder click, then . . . "Hello?" An older male voice answered.

David cleared his throat once more. "Yes . . . may I speak to Wesley Horton?" he asked nervously.

"This is Wes Horton," the voice replied.

David hoped this person would be more helpful.

"I'm sorry to bother you," David began politely, "but was your grandfather's name . . ."

Almost forgetting, David quickly turned to the sheet of paper. He put his finger under a name at the bottom of the list.

"Ron Horton?" David read the name aloud and at the same time finished his question.

"Yes, that's right," the voice answered.

"Don't worry, Mr. Horton, I'm not trying to sell you anything," David said, attempting to hide his nervousness. "My name is David Barnes. I just want to ask you a couple of questions about your grandfather."

"Sure," Mr. Horton answered. "But what is this for?" The voice seemed a bit more comfortable, which helped put David at ease.

From where he was, David heard the front door open. Then he heard his mother's voice. "Hi, Joe. Hello, Wishbone," she said. "David and Sam are in the kitchen."

Almost forgetting Mr. Horton's question, David quickly turned his attention back to his phone call. "Uh . . . actually," he said, "some friends and I are doing research on the Oakdale Oaks."

Joe and Wishbone entered the kitchen. Joe started to greet them, but Sam quickly put a finger to her lips and pointed to David. David waved, then angled his body slightly away from them as he turned his attention back to the phone conversation.

"I'm sure I can help you," the voice said. "Gramps used to tell us all about his baseball days." The voice was getting a bit excited. "Did you know he got to be

on three different teams during his time in the Negro
League?"

David was becoming nervous. He was getting
close to asking the really important question. "That's
great, Mr. Horton." *Here it comes,* David thought. "But I
was wondering if you could tell me about his days in
Oakdale."

David waited. Would Mr. Horton be like the
others?

"Oakdale?" the voice answered angrily.

Yes, it seemed as if Wesley Horton would be like
all the rest.

"There's a real neighborly town for you!" he said
in a sarcastic tone. "Why, I wouldn't set foot in Oakdale
if you paid me!" Mr. Horton continued angrily. "Not
after what that town did to my grandfather!"

David quickly tried to save the conversation from ending. "I'm sorry, Mr. Horton," he said quickly, "I'm calling from Oakdale—"

"You are *calling* from Oakdale?" the angry voice interrupted.

David would bet his entire computer system on what was coming next. "Yes, but—"

Click! And he would have won.

David sighed as he placed the phone back onto the wall. He looked at Sam. "Just like the others," he told her. Sam sighed and closed the rest of the open books in front of her.

"*What's* just like the others?" Joe asked with interest. Even Wishbone seemed concerned as he placed his front paws on Sam's legs. She gave him a quick rub behind the ears.

Sam quickly answered. "We've called four different families of the original players . . ."

David quickly took over the conversation. "Whenever I mention that I'm from the town of Oakdale, they won't talk to me."

Joe's jaw dropped from the news. "I don't believe it," he said.

"Believe it, Joe," David said. "In fact, this last guy said he would never set foot in Oakdale after what the town did to his grandfather."

"I don't get it," Sam remarked. "What did *Oakdale* do to him?" She closed the last of her books and dropped a hand back to Wishbone's ear.

"Whatever it is," Joe said, "I bet it has something to do with the missing year."

David agreed. The Oaks, the missing newspapers,

the anger shown by the players' families—it was all too much of a coincidence.

"Well, there wasn't anything out of the ordinary about the Oaks in these Negro League books we checked out of the library. There were accounts of the championship, but that's it. The answer has to be in those newspapers."

"Or in the town history," Joe added. Then he asked, "Do you two remember the Oakdale history book we used for social studies?"

"Yes," David and Sam said, almost at once.

Joe continued. "Well, Mrs. McKinley was telling me how she remembered reading something about the Oakdale Oaks in it."

David was excited by the news. Now, maybe they would get to the bottom of the mystery.

"So, let's go to the library and check out a copy," Sam said. "I have to return all of these books anyway." She began to stuff them into her backpack. David and Joe also filled their backpacks with the books.

David slung his pack over his shoulder. "Well, I'm definitely ready to get away from the telephone for a while," he said with a sigh.

Wishbone came up to David and nosed his leg. The boy knelt down and patted the dog's head.

"I hope your day's been better than mine has, Wishbone," David said.

The dog's tail wagged in what seemed like a reply. Scientific studies had claimed that petting a dog or cat could make a person feel better. As David stroked Wishbone's back, he relaxed. He believed there was some truth to the theory.

The three kids went outside, got on their bikes, and rode to the library. Wishbone took the lead.

As they rode, David thought back to the upsetting phone calls. The good feeling he had gotten from petting Wishbone slowly left him. Why did those people have such a problem with Oakdale? And why were they upset with him? They didn't even know him. Yet they didn't want to talk to him because of the town he lived in. David didn't think that was right.

He wondered about the Negro League. It was a league that was *created* by prejudice. He wondered why anyone would object to playing on a team with someone of a different color. He wondered why anyone would not want to watch or own a team that had players of different colors. The whole idea seemed ridiculous to him, no matter how many times he thought about it.

Being an African-American, David knew his ancestors' history quite well. He was no stranger to stories of slavery, segregation, and racial prejudice. He knew the stories well, but he never really experienced anything close to it—until today. He wondered if the people he talked to would have treated him differently if they knew he was the same color they were. Maybe . . .

As they approached the library, David was grateful he lived in a town where no one judged him by something as unimportant as the color of his skin.

Chapter Seven

Wishbone watched as David, Sam, and Joe each entered the library. He hesitated, still feeling a little strange being allowed inside. After all, until just recently, if Wishbone wanted to help Joe find a book or help himself to the microfiche machine, he had to *sneak* in. Fortunately, that had changed. As long as no one complained, he could stay.

Wishbone followed everyone in. Once again, the cool air felt good on his damp nose. They all walked toward the main office. Joe gave a light knock on the open door to announce their arrival. Wishbone zigzagged between legs to get a look inside.

What he saw was Ellen Talbot sitting at her desk—a desk that was covered with long, slender microfiche file drawers. Any part of the desk that wasn't covered by the drawers held stacks of the little microfiche folders. Ellen was probably searching through every folder for the missing year's worth of newspapers. From the look of frustration on her face, it appeared she had been searching for a long time. Ellen quickly glanced at the kids and Wishbone as they approached.

"Are you okay, Mom?" Joe asked. "I thought you were going to come home for lunch."

"I had to work through lunch, Joe," Ellen replied. As she spoke, she grabbed a handful of microfiche folders and replaced them into one of the drawers. "I'm just hoping that 1933 was misfiled by accident."

"Now this mystery is making people miss meals!" Wishbone said. "What's this world coming to?"

"I don't think 1933 is missing by accident," David said. David went on to tell Ellen about all the phone calls he had made. He described how each of the people reacted when they learned he was from Oakdale.

"That's terrible, David," Ellen replied after hearing how he was treated. "What could have made them dislike Oakdale so much?"

"We think we may be able to find out," Sam said hopefully.

"I went to see Mrs. McKinley," Joe explained. "She reminded me of a book I used in social studies class last year—a book about Oakdale history."

"I think I know that book," Ellen said, getting up from her desk chair. She led the kids out of her office and to the front counter. "Let's look it up on the computer."

Wishbone watched as Ellen entered something into the computer. He thought computers would be great if they would just be made with bigger keyboards, so he could punch in information. The ones that existed now were just too small for his paws to handle!

"Here it is," Ellen said finally. She read the title off the screen. "*Oakdale—A Little Town with a Big History.* We have three copies," Ellen continued. "One is a first edition, and two are third editions." She pointed to the screen. "It looks as if they're all in. The Dewey decimal number is: 976.42812 STE."

As she read the number, Joe wrote it down on one of the slips of paper nearby.

"You're in luck," she said. "The old, first edition was just checked in yesterday." Ellen left the counter and headed back to her office. "Good luck," she said. "It's back to the microfiche search for me."

"Thanks, Mrs. Talbot," Sam said politely.

With Joe in the lead, the kids made their way to the history section of the library. As they went, they passed Mr. Carroll and his book-filled table. He was there again, in the same spot they'd seen him the day before.

I wonder if that guy ever goes home, Wishbone thought.

The man was reading a large book that he held up in front of him. But as the kids and Wishbone passed by, Mr. Carroll seemed to be watching the dog more than reading his book.

"Uh-oh," Wishbone said. "He's probably not a dog lover." Wishbone tried to blend in with the kids in front of him. "Don't mind me," he said. "I'm not a dog. I'm . . . I'm . . . just a really short kid . . . with a lot of hair and a tail!"

When the group got to the history section, Joe and the others carefully examined the shelves of books and scanned their spines until they found a match. They saw two copies of the history book. Joe removed both from the shelf and handed one to Sam. Without saying a word, both Joe and Sam began to thumb through the books in search of anything about the Oaks. Out of the corner of his eye, Joe saw David continuing to look across the shelves.

"Joe, didn't your mom say there were three copies of the book?" David asked.

"Yes," Joe answered, still flipping through the pages of his copy. "They're all the same, though, aren't they?"

"Well, actually—" David began to say. Then he was interrupted by Sam.

"Here they are!" Sam said excitedly. Both Joe and David leaned over her shoulder to get a better look. Even Wishbone seemed to be interested as he raised himself up and placed his front two paws on Joe's leg. Joe checked the page number at the bottom of Sam's book. Then he flipped to the same page in the book he was holding.

"It doesn't look like there's very much written about them," David said from his position over Sam's shoulder.

"There's just a couple of pages," Joe added, as he reached the same section in his book.

"I don't see anything unusual written about them," Sam said. "There's certainly not anything to make it worth hiding an entire year's worth of news items."

"Let's try to find the first edition," David said. "Sometimes things are changed in later editions when other items are added, or when new facts disagree with old ones."

The kids turned their attention back to the spot where they had found the other two copies. They searched carefully, but the first edition of the history book wasn't there. Joe even checked the Dewey decimal number again. He also looked at the numbers on the books that were supposed to be on either side of the Oakdale history book. It was definitely the right spot, but no book was there to match the number.

"Maybe someone was looking at it in the reading area and left it on a table," Sam said. Sam left the boys for a moment and walked over to the tables to see if she could spot the book there.

"Maybe someone put it back on the shelf in the wrong place," David said, scanning the nearby books.

Joe did the same. Then he checked the entire row, then the next one, then the next one. Nothing.

"It's not on any of the tables," Sam said as she returned. "It's not even with any of the books Mr. Carroll is using. I asked him."

"We're hoping it got returned to the wrong part of the history section," David said, still scanning shelves. Sam joined in to help the boys look.

"You two keep checking around here," Joe told Sam and David. "I'm going to check with my mom again."

Joe walked back to the front counter, with Wishbone at his side. As Joe approached the counter, he saw Ellen assisting a young girl. She handed the girl two books. Then the girl turned and walked out of the library.

Joe took the girl's place at the counter. "She didn't happen to check out that history book about Oakdale, did she, Mom?" Joe asked.

"No," Ellen answered. "Why do you ask?"

"Well, we found the two later editions, but we can't find the first edition anywhere," Joe said with some frustration in his voice.

"Well, I was positive . . ." Ellen began to say, as she moved to the computer once more. She typed in the name of the book and examined the screen. "It should be here," she said. "No one has checked it out, and it shows here that it was returned yesterday."

Sam and David approached the counter. "We've checked the whole section," Sam told them.

David finished the thought. "We can't find it anywhere."

"But you found the other two copies?" Ellen asked.

"Yes, but we think the first edition may have some

information that the later editions don't have," David told her.

"Let me call the *Chronicle*," Ellen said. She walked toward her office. "Maybe Wanda owns a first edition."

Joe thought something was vaguely familiar about the situation. Then it hit him! It was too coincidental! Too convenient! It was just like the bloody thumbprint!

In "The Adventure of the Norwood Builder," the murder suspect, who happened to be Sherlock Holmes's client, John McFarlane, was placed in a serious situation because of the huge amount of evidence found against him for the murder of Jonas Oldacre. After searching the murder scene, even Holmes himself was beginning to think McFarlane was guilty as well. But Holmes changed his mind when the police found a final and airtight piece of evidence against McFarlane—a bloody thumbprint. McFarlane's bloody thumbprint!

Holmes went to investigate the thumbprint the next day. It had been found behind a jacket hanging on a wall rack in Jonas Oldacre's house. To everyone else, it proved McFarlane's guilt beyond a shadow of a doubt. But to Sherlock Holmes, it proved the exact *opposite*. It proved that McFarlane was innocent of murder!

Sherlock Holmes remembered checking the spot where the print was found the day before. On the day before, it hadn't been there. Its strange, sudden appearance only proved all the more that someone was trying to frame John McFarlane for murder.

Joe thought the missing Oakdale history book was his and his friends' version of the bloody thumbprint.

Someone knew that the kids were looking for the missing year! That same person must have stolen the first edition of the history book! There had to be a major clue inside that history book—something that would have been edited out of the later editions. Something in that particular book would tell them why anyone would want to steal a year's worth of newspapers.

Ellen stepped out of her office and made her way to the counter. "They only have third editions at the *Chronicle*," she told the kids, "same as we have here."

"What do we do now?" Sam asked.

Everyone stood in silence for a moment. Joe looked down at Wishbone, who gave his tail a quick wag in response to Joe's glance.

Joe's thoughts wandered to the next part of the Sherlock Holmes mystery. He also began to think about Holmes's solution to the mystery.

"I think I have an idea," Joe said with a smile.

Chapter Eight

As the kids and Wishbone entered the offices of *The Oakdale Chronicle,* Joe was immediately swept up in the noise of a busy office building. The *Chronicle* itself was basically one long, open room. Everyone employed there worked side by side. On the main floor and to the kids' right, workers sat at rows of desks, writing and editing the news for the next issue. To their left, graphic artists sat at drafting tables working on the newspaper's design and layout.

At the opposite end of the main floor, a short flight of steps led up to Wanda's office, which was a loft that overlooked the work area. There was another short flight of steps that ran down from the main floor, into a sunken area where a few rows of filing cabinets, supplies, and other items were stored. At the far right of this area was another set of steps that ran down to the basement.

Joe walked up the steps and came into Wanda's open office. "Can we go down to the archives, Miss Gilmore?" Joe asked.

Wanda was typing. She responded by nodding and waving one hand, without looking up. She seemed to be deep in concentration. "You go ahead. I'll be right with you," she finally said.

The kids went on ahead. They walked down into the sunken storage area. Next, they proceeded down the long, dimly lit staircase that led to the basement. Joe led the way as he, Sam, David and Wishbone walked down the steps. Once at the bottom, Joe flicked the switch that he saw Wanda use another time when they were at the *Chronicle*'s offices. The fluorescent lights fluttered on with a soft buzz. The kids found themselves among the rows of shelves holding all the *Chronicle*'s back issues.

"*Now* are you going to tell us why we're here?" David asked impatiently.

"Well," Joe began, "I've been reading this Sherlock Holmes book. One of the stories in it reminded me of the mystery we have here."

Joe explained how Holmes was asked to clear Mr. McFarlane's name, but that he couldn't find a way to do so until the appearance of the thumbprint. It was Holmes's clue that someone was trying to frame McFarlane.

Joe continued: "So Sherlock Holmes suspected there might not even have been a murder in the first place."

"What does that have to do with the missing 1933 newspapers?" Sam asked.

"Miss Gilmore said that it would be very difficult for anyone to actually steal whole boxes full of newspapers," Joe explained. "So what if there wasn't a theft at all? Suppose this whole mystery is just the same as when Holmes suspected there wasn't really a murder?"

David seemed frustrated. "But we've already looked for the newspapers," he said. "They're not here."

Wishbone gave a short bark. Everyone turned to see someone's legs walking down the staircase. It was Wanda.

"So, kids," she began, "do you have a happy ending for my front-page story?"

"We just may, Miss Gilmore," Joe replied. Then he explained to her about the relationship between the Holmes short story and the missing year of papers.

"So how did Sherlock Holmes solve the case?" Sam asked, as Joe finished summing up the story.

"Well," he began, "Sherlock Holmes counted the paces it took to walk from one end of the inside of Mr. Oldacre's house to the other. He then went outside and measured the length again. The number of paces from inside the house were less than the number of paces from the outside."

"So . . ." Sam almost had the mystery figured out.

"So there had to be a secret room inside the house! The inside measured less than the outside," David said quickly.

Joe finished his explanation. "It turned out that Jonas Oldacre wasn't murdered after all. He was hiding in a secret room the whole time." Everyone seemed satisfied with the solution. Joe continued.

"He had framed John McFarlane for his own murder. It seemed Oldacre hated the McFarlane family, so he had framed McFarlane in order to punish him and get revenge."

"So you don't think the boxes were ever stolen?" Wanda asked.

"Maybe not," Joe said. Then he asked Wanda a question. "When was the *Chronicle* originally founded, Miss Gilmore?"

"It was established in 1926," she answered promptly.

"And how many boxes does a year's worth of newspapers take up?" Joe asked.

"Each year takes up about three boxes," Wanda answered.

David came in with the math. "So there should be seventy-two years' worth of newspapers in here, for a total of two hundred and sixteen boxes!"

"*If* all of the newspapers are really here," Sam added quickly.

"All we have to do is count the total boxes and see if the year was even stolen," Joe concluded.

"Well, don't just stand there!" Wanda said excitedly. "Let's start counting boxes!"

Wishbone had to take a couple of steps back. "Whoa!" he said. "Look at that dust fly!" He watched as the kids and Wanda each took a row of shelves and started counting boxes.

"Wish I could help, guys," Wishbone said, his tail

wagging. "But when dust clogs my nose, I can barely sniff." *And what's a dog without a good sniffer?*

With everyone searching, it didn't take long to count every box. Everyone took their totals to David. He added them up in his head.

"Two hundred and sixteen," he said to everyone. "That's how many boxes are here—and that's how many boxes *should* be here." Everyone looked at one another in surprise.

"But how?" Wanda asked.

"We checked all of the dates yesterday," Sam added. "There were no duplications."

"All I know," David said, "is that if the year 1933 was actually missing, we should have counted only two hundred and thirteen boxes."

Seeing that the dust was beginning to settle, Wishbone trotted over to join the group. Something suddenly caught his sense of smell. It wasn't a strange aroma. It just smelled out of place. With his nose to the ground, he walked over to the closest shelf. In fact, the scent didn't smell out of place in the archives, just out of place in this section. He inspected the shelf a bit closer.

"A-choo!" the little terrier sneezed.

As Wishbone gave the shelf a good sniffing, he realized he was in the oldest section of the archives. That was why most of the dust seemed to be hanging out over there. Then it occurred to him what seemed out of place. He was in the oldest section, but there was a not-so-very-old smell on some of the boxes. Wishbone barked, trying to get Joe's attention. "Hey, Joe! Over here!"

"What are you barking at, Wishbone?" Joe asked as he went over to the dog. When he got to where Wishbone was, Joe knelt and looked around. Wishbone kept barking.

"Come on, Joe," the dog said, still barking. "It's right there in front of you!" When Joe's eyes widened, Wishbone knew Joe had finally spotted what he had just smelled. His pal's hand reached out and touched the clean white label on one of the boxes. Wishbone stopped barking, relieved that Joe had picked up on the clue that he had pointed out.

"Miss Gilmore," Joe said without looking away from the boxes. "What year did you say the *Chronicle* was established?"

"In 1926, Joe," she answered. "Why?"

Wishbone stepped back as Joe pulled one of the heavy boxes off the lower shelf. "Because, it looks like there's . . ."—he touched the labels of two other boxes—"one . . . two . . . three boxes here from the year 1925."

"*What?*" Wanda gasped. She, Sam, and David immediately rushed over to check out Joe's discovery. "That *can't* be right!"

"It looks like someone relabeled these old boxes with fake, new labels that say 1925," Joe explained. He pointed to one of the boxes. "See? These labels aren't yellowed and faded like the other ones in this section."

Joe then carefully opened one box and pulled out an edition of one of the old papers. He held up the folded newspaper, letting the bottom half flop down. Looking at the top of the front page, he read the date that was printed there. "July 26, 1933!" he said with a smile.

"You found the missing year!" Sam said excitedly.

"No—Wishbone found it," Joe replied.

Wishbone gave a small bark. "Hey!" he said. "The nose always knows!"

Chapter Nine

Sitting upstairs in Wanda's office, Wishbone heard nothing but the rustling of newspapers. Everyone had an old 1933 edition of the *Chronicle* and was scanning it for anything about the Oakdale Oaks. Wanda was reading one paper at her desk. David and Sam had their heads buried in newspapers at Wanda's couch. Joe sat in a nearby chair reading another newspaper from 1933.

"Here's something," David said, breaking the silence. "It's about some new Oaks team members." Everyone looked up for a moment. Then they went back to their own paper. It seemed to Wishbone that articles about the Oaks were good, but nothing was as important as finding out why someone would have hidden the newspapers in the first place. Wishbone wanted to know this, as well. After all, dogs and newspapers had a long history together.

"Here's an interview with Lindsay Groves himself!" Joe said excitedly. He carried it over to Wanda's desk, where Sam and David joined him. Wishbone placed his front paws up on the desk to get a better look.

There on the page, next to the article, Wishbone saw a photograph of Lindsay Groves. This one was different from the one on Joe's baseball card. This was a picture of Groves in mid-pitch. Wishbone could see Legion Field's outfield in the background. "Hey!" he said. "That's the place where I catch all the fly balls. And I do mean *all* of them!"

"It says here," Joe began, "that Lindsay Groves has deep family roots in Jefferson."

"That's practically right next door to Oakdale," Sam said. "I wonder if he still lives there."

"It sure would be cool to meet him," David said. Then he returned to the couch. "But I'm sure there's nothing in that article that would make someone want to hide the newspapers."

"I'm sure you're right," Sam replied. She, too, went back to the couch and picked up her newspaper.

Joe was still excited about the find. "Can I make a copy of this?" he asked Wanda.

"Sure, Joe," she answered. "The copy machine is just downstairs."

Wishbone watched through the railing as Joe ran downstairs and hurriedly made a copy of the Groves article. He had a feeling that Joe wanted to read the article thoroughly later, when he could take his time. But the urgency in Joe's movements now told Wishbone that, more important, Joe wanted to get back to the newspaper search.

Sam finished reading her issue of the *Chronicle*. She placed it on top of a stack near the white box where she had gotten it. Then she reached inside the box and pulled out another newspaper.

This was a complete puzzle. She couldn't think of anything so terrible that someone would want to hide it from the rest of the world. Actually, she couldn't think of anything terrible happening at all in Oakdale. It just didn't seem possible. The unanswered questions just made Sam search even harder.

She read through her entire issue and found nothing relating to the Oakdale Oaks. It seemed David had the same bad luck as he folded up his copy, as well. They both placed their papers neatly onto the "already read" stack. Each one took a new copy of the *Chronicle* out of the box.

Next to Sam, David unfolded his paper and quickly called out, "Check it out—front page!" Everyone turned to see David holding up a paper with a headline that read "Oaks Become National Champs!"

Joe rushed over to get a closer look. Even Wishbone trotted over, his tail wagging.

"I almost forgot why we started this whole search," Joe said happily.

Sam glanced over David's shoulder. The article had a team photograph along with it. Sam decided to let Joe and David scan that article. She began to unfold her own paper. She didn't think anyone would hide a year's worth of newspapers simply because a team won the national championship.

As Sam opened her newspaper and read the headline, she knew for certain that she had found something really important.

"Guys, I think I found what we've been looking for!" Sam held up the newspaper, and then handed it to Joe.

"'A Foul Play in Oakdale!'" Joe read the big headline aloud.

"What?" Wanda asked, rising from her desk.

There was a short pause. Then Joe went on. "The article is written by Giles Gilmore himself."

Everyone crowded around Joe and silently read the article. As Sam read, she reached over and scratched Wishbone behind the ears.

In the article, Gilmore explained how everything

was set to go for the Oakdale Oaks victory parade down Oak Street. Then, all of a sudden, the town council canceled the parade due to zoning restrictions. Gilmore went on to point out how other parades had been held under similar situations, but there were no "zoning restrictions" mentioned then.

Gilmore's article continued, accusing the town council of being racially prejudiced against the Oaks. He even accused them of never even planning to hold the parade in the first place. If the Oaks lost, no parade. If the Oaks won, no parade because of zoning restrictions. Gilmore then claimed that no one in town—other than himself—seemed to be willing to stand up for the Oaks.

All in all, the article was a very strong attack—not only against the town council, but against the indifference of most of the town's residents, as well.

"I don't believe it." David was the first to speak, and he took the words right out of Sam's mouth. "Did this *really* happen?"

"If Dad wrote it," Wanda said, almost in shock herself, "you can be sure it happened."

Everyone was silent as the ugly truth sank in. Like David, Sam couldn't believe it. It seemed almost impossible that something terrible like this could have happened in the town they lived in, no matter how long ago it was. Was Giles Gilmore right? Did the town council members not give the Oaks a parade just because of the color of their skin? The idea of it was completely outrageous to Sam.

"I don't believe it," David repeated.

"This has to be the reason," Joe said quietly. "This

has to be why someone tried to hide all of the 1933 newspapers."

"Someone didn't want people to remember this part of Oakdale's history," Wanda added.

"That's why none of the players or their families wanted to talk to us once they found out we were from Oakdale," David added quietly.

Suddenly, an idea occurred to Sam. "Let's see what was written in the following issues." Each of the group reached into the white box and pulled out issues of the *Chronicle* that followed the one they had just read.

Sam pulled out the issue that was next in the sequence of dates. She opened it and looked at the front page. "'Injustice to the Oaks,'" she said aloud, reading that day's headline.

"'Oaks Deserve Parade,'" David said, reading another headline from his paper.

They both looked at Joe. He just shrugged his shoulders and held up his issue. "'Highway Bill Is a Go,'" he quoted.

Sam turned back to her article. Joe, David, and Wanda gathered around Sam. Skimming her paper quickly, they discovered the article was about the town council meeting at which Giles Gilmore spoke on behalf of the Oaks. He directly attacked the town council's motives for enforcing the new "zoning restrictions." However, in the end, the Oaks were still denied their parade.

"What about your paper, David?" Sam asked.

David flipped his *Chronicle* open. This time, everyone read over *his* shoulder. The article in his paper seemed to be made up of personal interviews with the

Oaks team members themselves. There were stories about the championship game, and the players' feelings about the parade's cancellation.

After scanning the article, Wanda stepped away from the kids and went over to the box where they had found the articles. She searched through several other issues, but she didn't find anything else about the parade. Joe searched other boxes.

Sam finished skimming through the article David found. It was interesting, but it didn't really give any new information. She turned to Joe and Wanda. "Are you finding anything else?" she asked them.

Both Wanda and Joe answered, "No."

"I found a short article about an exhibition game," Joe said. "But that's it."

"Why would the coverage stop after only three articles?" Wanda asked, pretty much to herself.

"Maybe Mr. Gilmore was wrong about what he thought was going on," David stated in a hopeful tone.

"If he had been wrong," Sam said, "wouldn't he have printed a retraction—an apology for making a mistake in his reporting?"

"That's right," Wanda agreed. "But I don't understand why he would have written such strongly worded attacks on the town council and then . . . that's the end of it."

"It's like a book without an ending," David added.

Joe stood and walked over to Wanda's desk. "What we need is a witness," Joe said, "someone who was around at the time all this happened—someone who was affected by the council's ruling." He picked up the copy he'd made of the Lindsay Groves article.

Chapter Ten

Joe pedaled harder as he rode up a small hill. When he reached the top, he saw Wishbone investigating a lamppost. The dog watched Joe's approach, gave one more sniff, then moved on. Behind him, Joe heard the sounds of Sam and David's bikes. Other than that, Joe heard little else on the nearly deserted road.

They were riding down a country road that led to the nearby town of Jefferson. Although the Wednesday morning air was cool, the summer sun was beginning to pour its warmth onto the four travelers. Luckily, the ride over to Jefferson was not a long trip.

Yesterday, David had been able to find Lindsay Groves's address and phone number on the Internet. Joe had then talked to him on the phone. Groves agreed to meet with the kids on Wednesday. He seemed to be very nice, even after Joe told him that he lived in Oakdale.

Ever since the kids had biked over the Oakdale town limits, everyone had kept fairly quiet. Even

Wishbone had remained unusually quiet—especially considering that this trip to a new place was quite an adventure for him. It was as if they all were thinking about the history lesson they had learned the day before. Joe certainly was. He found it very hard to believe that such an ugly racial incident could have happened in his hometown.

But, then again, the Oakdale Oaks were a Negro League team. The very existence of their team was clear proof that separation of the races existed back then. Joe figured that it wasn't a big step to go from separate leagues to no parade for blacks.

What if it really hadn't happened that way, though? What if the accusations made by Giles Gilmore were just that—accusations, and not hard facts? After all, if the incident really did happen, and if Gilmore was so upset about it, why did he write only three articles on the subject? The question gave Joe a little hope for the integrity of his town. It was a lot easier to believe that one man might have gotten the wrong idea or lied about something, rather than to believe that a whole town council and residents would prevent a parade from taking place because of the color of certain people's skin.

But why would Giles Gilmore deliberately lie? And if it wasn't a lie, how could a journalist of his reputation make such a terrible error in his reporting and writing?

Behind Joe, David continued to pedal his bike in silence. After David found out about the canceled parade, the only thing he felt sure about was the fact that he wasn't really sure how he felt! Part of him was very hurt and disappointed. He couldn't believe he lived in a town where something like that could have happened.

Certainly, all this happened a long time ago. But, then again, it wasn't *that* long ago—it was still the twentieth century. It was bad enough that town council members were prejudiced against the Oaks. But how could the townspeople of Oakdale let something like that happen?

That thought brought David to the other emotion he was feeling: anger. David was angry at the town council members of that time period. He was also angry at the townspeople. It was bad enough that members of the Oaks were forced to play in an entirely different league from white ball players. But when those same players won the national championship, they weren't even allowed the dignity and joy of walking down Oak Street in front of their fans.

Until today, racial prejudice in Oakdale would never have crossed his mind. Never would he have imagined people living in Oakdale would look down on other people simply because of the color of their skin—or for any other reason, either. But they used to feel that way years ago. So why not now?

Why would Giles Gilmore write those three articles, then nothing more? He didn't seem like the type of person who would just give up when there wasn't anyone else to support him. But it did seem that, in fact, Gilmore did give up. He didn't write any more articles about the injustice shown toward the Oaks.

Joe took a right and turned down a street on the outskirts of Jefferson. David followed him and was gradually drawn back into the events of the present time. Maybe Lindsay Groves could answer some of his questions.

Behind David, Sam rode her bicycle in silence, as well. She, too, was troubled by what they had found out yesterday. It seemed that their view of Oakdale had been shattered.

To them, the Oakdale they lived in was home to people who cared about and helped one another—no matter who the people were. It wasn't a town full of prejudiced residents. And it certainly wasn't a town full of people who would just sit around quietly and do nothing when someone else was being treated unfairly. At least, that was the Oakdale they lived in now. Sam had automatically thought that her hometown had always been that way. Now she was beginning to think she might be wrong.

The articles they found, however, didn't affect her nearly as much as they did David. Ever since they learned the shocking news, David seemed very upset and distant. He had gone straight home from the *Chronicle* offices, saying he wanted to be alone. Today, he had been very quiet during the trip over to Jefferson. It was as if he seemed to feel the articles were personal attacks on him and his heritage.

Sam understood why the articles would hit closer to home for David. But she didn't think he should take the situation so personally. After all, it was not as if something like that could happen in their modern-day town of Oakdale. . . . Or could it?

Ahead, Sam saw Joe and Wishbone turn right into the driveway of a small, one-story, faded-blue house. David and Sam quickly followed. In the driveway, they parked their bikes. Then they went up to the front door.

Joe knocked. An elderly gentleman opened the door. He was a tall, thin man, dressed in a brown shirt and pants. Sam could easily spot the resemblance between the young man pictured on Joe's baseball card and the face of the aging, gray-haired man standing in front of her now. His eyes hadn't changed at all. They still seemed to hold the same determination that the eyes of the younger Lindsay Groves had held.

"You must be the kids from Oakdale," the older man said. He held open the door with his left hand and extended his right. "I'm Lindsay Groves."

The kids, each in turn, shook Mr. Groves's hand and introduced themselves. Wishbone proudly trotted up to him, sat down, and extended a paw of his own.

Lindsay Groves looked down at Wishbone. "Howdy, little fella," he said. "I'd bend down and shake your paw, but I probably wouldn't be able to get up again." He gave a smile and a wink to the kids. They laughed softly.

"That's my dog, Wishbone," Joe said nervously.

Sam was getting the feeling that Wishbone was as excited as they were to meet the former ball player.

"Pleased to meet you, Mr. Wishbone," Mr. Groves greeted the dog.

Wishbone gave a bark in reply, almost as if he understood.

"Come on in," Mr. Groves said. He stepped onto the porch to hold open the door. "You, too, Mr. Wishbone."

Once everyone was inside, Mr. Groves led them to what looked like an old parlor room. Almost immediately, the kids and Wishbone noticed that one wall was completely covered with old baseball items and souvenirs. There were old photographs and old newspaper articles, including the one Joe had made a copy of the day before. All of them were yellowed with age. There was also a cabinet full of old trophies, gloves, and signed baseballs. Sam even saw a framed baseball card, just like the one Joe had.

Sam and Wishbone were the first to take a seat in the small room, which seemed more like a museum. It took Joe and David a bit longer to tear themselves away from all of the baseball mementos.

After everyone was seated, Mr. Groves started the conversation. "So, you kids have a couple of questions for an old ball player."

"We sure do," Joe said eagerly.

"Did the Oakdale town council really cancel your victory parade after you won the national championship because the Oaks were black?" David asked immediately. Sam was surprised at David's upfront line of questioning.

"You're not shy about getting right to the point, are you, David?" Mr. Groves replied with a small laugh.

"You see," Joe added quickly, "we found some old newspaper articles, written by Giles Gilmore of the *Chronicle,* about how he suspected that—"

"I know those articles very well, Joe," Groves interrupted. "And to be quite honest, we team members of the Oaks agreed with Giles Gilmore. We thought the Oakdale town council canceled the parade just because of our color."

Sam was shocked to hear the news. She guessed that part of her was wishing Giles Gilmore had been wrong about his accusations. She looked at Joe and David. She could tell by their disappointed faces that they were hoping for the same thing.

"Then why did Mr. Gilmore print just those three articles, then nothing else?" Joe asked.

"If what he wrote in his articles was true," David added, "why did he stop fighting?"

"He never stopped fighting," Mr. Groves said. "Why, those articles alone almost made him lose his newspaper. Many of his advertisers, distributors, and subscribers were all ready to drop him and wash their hands of him. The town council was even pushing for him to print a retraction, but he wouldn't do it."

Groves leaned back against the couch, then continued. "The most anyone could get Gilmore to do was drop the subject and not print any more stories about the cancellation of the parade. By then, many of the Oaks ball players were angry. I don't think most of them would have shown up for the parade—if there had finally been one."

The kids just listened in silence while Groves continued.

"Gilmore took a big chance by writing those articles in the first place. He almost ended up paying for his views by losing his livelihood."

In Lindsay Groves's house, Wishbone took in a flood of new smells. It seemed like the longer a person was around, the more different kinds of smells their house would accumulate over the years.

Wishbone was drawn to all the cool stuff in the parlor. He wished the gloves and balls weren't inside a cabinet, though. There was no telling how many great scents those items still had. However, everything at or below nose level had plenty of interesting aromas, as well. Wishbone made himself busy sniffing as Mr. Groves continued his story.

"Did Giles Gilmore just give up?" David asked.

"No," Groves answered. "Giles Gilmore never really gave up. He just became very clever. You see, he and the *Chronicle* became the biggest supporters of the Oakdale Oaks after that incident with the parade. He overhauled the playing field. He printed all of the baseball programs and baseball cards, and he paid for all the printing out of his own pocket. He even had *The Oakdale Chronicle* become the team's official sponsor."

Lindsay Groves leaned forward and stared up at the ceiling, thinking some more about the old days.

Then he said to the kids, "I tell you what—the time I spent playing for the Oaks was some of the best years of my life."

Wishbone stopped sniffing and sat down by the chair Joe was sitting in. He looked up to the baseball wall. He saw all the photos of Groves in his prime, playing at Legion Field. Then, suddenly, out of no-where, Wishbone had a craving for hot dogs and popcorn.

"Weren't you upset at all about the cancellation of the parade?" David asked. To Wishbone, David still seemed to be upset.

"Oh," Lindsay Groves answered, "I suppose I was angry. But, then again, a Negro League team having its own parade through downtown Oakdale was a bit of wishful thinking back in those days. You know, David, you're lucky to be living in an Oakdale where that sort of thing doesn't happen anymore."

"Yes," David replied, "I suppose so." But Wish-bone sensed that David wasn't completely convinced.

"I tell you," Lindsay Groves said, changing the subject, "we did have a grand old time, though. In our part of town, where the black folks lived, we were treated like celebrities!" He pointed to the wall of memories and let out a sigh. "It definitely was a special time for baseball. Why, for that period in time, two big leagues ran parallel to each other. The major leagues had Babe Ruth. We blacks had Josh Gibson and Leroy 'Satchel' Paige, and he was one of the greatest pitchers of all time—regardless of color."

Lindsay Groves pulled his hands to his chest and looked over both shoulders, as if he were preparing to pitch an imaginary ball.

"You know," he continued, "some people used to say that 'Satchel' Paige had more victories during his time pitching than any other pitcher in the whole history of baseball."

Groves let his hands drop to his lap, but his eyes were still full of excitement.

"They also say that Josh Gibson was the only man ever to hit a ball completely out of Yankee Stadium! They called that stadium 'the house that Ruth built.' But even Babe Ruth couldn't hit a ball out of there." Groves let out a small chuckle.

"Did you ever get to play with Paige or Gibson?" Joe asked. Wishbone could tell his pal was wrapped up in the excitement of the stories.

"I never played *with* them," Groves replied. "But I played *against* them many times, while the Oaks were barnstorming."

"What's barnstorming?" David asked.

"That was when Negro League teams would travel around the country and play a combination of small-town teams, all-star teams, or even major-league teams," Groves explained.

"Those were the exhibition games we read about in the *Chronicle*," Sam added.

"Sure," the old ball player agreed. "Why, we even *won* most of the games when we played against the major-league teams. It wasn't because black players were any better than the white players. We just felt, being in a segregated league, that we had to go all out to prove ourselves. So, during those games, we hit a little harder and we ran a little faster."

Lindsay Groves let out a small sigh before going on with his stories.

Then he said, "Yep, the magic of the Negro League

went on from around 1920 until 1947. That was when Jackie Robinson—the most well known black player of his day—broke the color barrier by being signed to the Brooklyn Dodgers. After 1947, baseball teams were integrated. Unfortunately, I figured I was already too far past my baseball prime, so to speak, to even try to go on to the major leagues at that point. But, you know what? I wouldn't trade my time in the Negro League for anything in the world."

As Groves spoke, Wishbone glanced, once again, at the trophy case. There, he saw something sitting on the floor behind it. The little dog walked over to the cabinet's base, hoping the object was what he thought it was.

"Uh-oh!" Wishbone said as he pulled the dusty baseball out from behind the case. "It looks as if Lindsay Groves let one get away from him." Proud of his discovery, Wishbone trotted over to Joe with the ball in his mouth.

Joe looked down to see what Wishbone was carrying. "Oh, no, Wishbone!" Joe cried. He reached down to take the baseball from the dog.

Wishbone relaxed his jaw as Joe carefully removed the baseball from his mouth. "Blech! Blech!" Wishbone said as some of the dust stuck to his tongue. "Don't worry, Joe. I wasn't going to chew it up or anything."

Joe looked toward Lindsay Groves. "I'm sorry, Mr. Groves," Joe said apologetically. "I'm sure this is a special game ball or something." He held out the ball to the older gentleman.

Mr. Groves carefully took the ball from Joe's hand

and looked at it closely. "Do you know what this is, Joe?"

"Uh-oh, here it comes," Wishbone said, as he put one paw over his nose.

"No, sir," Joe replied nervously. Sam and David seemed to be holding their breath.

Mr. Groves smiled. "One dollar and ninety-nine cents—on sale at the sporting goods store in town."

Everyone let out a huge sigh of relief. Wishbone put down his paw and wagged his tail. "I didn't think it tasted *that* important!"

"This ball probably belonged to my great-grandson, Joshua," Groves explained. He held out the ball to Wishbone. "Here you go, Mr. Wishbone. Josh has at least eight others just like this one."

Wow! This has really been my week, Wishbone thought, as he took the ball from Mr. Groves. "Say, Joe! Are there any more people's houses you want to go visit? I'm always on the lookout for new treasures to add to my collection."

As Lindsay Groves told the kids other stories about playing for the Oaks, Wishbone chewed on the now not-so-dusty baseball. Like the gift Mrs. McKinley had given him, the baseball could use a bit of dirt seasoning, until it tasted just right.

But as he continued to chew, Wishbone wondered if his new treasure would be safe in his usual hiding place. Up until now, whoever was digging up his valuable finds was taking only the bones. But that all could change. Soon, maybe nothing would be safe in what Wishbone had thought was the safest hiding place in all of Oakdale—Wanda's yard.

Chapter Eleven

As the three kids biked back to Oakdale, while Wishbone trotted in the lead, the early-afternoon sun beat down on their backs. Joe played back the day's events in his mind. They had met Lindsay Groves, one of the original Oakdale Oaks! He had entertained them for a long time with his stories of life as a baseball player in the Negro League. Even more important than that, he had explained that Giles Gilmore's articles about the parade cancellation were true.

That had been a huge sore spot with all of them, especially David. As odd as it might seem, the incident didn't bother Mr. Groves very much. Joe, however, was still left with a bad feeling about what had occurred. Sam seemed to feel the same way.

Wishbone was definitely in a good mood. Joe watched as his dog ran just ahead of their bikes. He had gotten the opportunity to investigate part of another town. Plus, he had gained a free baseball in the process! Joe thought Wishbone was very lucky to be a dog sometimes. At least other dogs didn't care about the color of one another's fur.

As the kids coasted down a large hill, Joe thought about the big question that was left unanswered: Who hid the missing material? Certainly, the year 1933 was a shameful period in Oakdale's past. However, was the racial incident worth losing an entire year of history?

Joe's thoughts turned to "The Adventure of the Norwood Builder." Sherlock Holmes knew that the key to the entire mystery was the appearance of the bloody thumbprint—and that print could be compared to the mystery of the Oakdale history book.

The disappearance of the history book had to be the key to finding out who hid the year's worth of 1933 newspapers. It was too much of a coincidence that the book went missing so soon after the kids started looking into the history of the Oaks. Whoever took the book, without checking it out of the library, probably knew what the kids were doing.

"I win! I win!" Wishbone said, as he was first to reach the library steps.

Joe, David, and Sam parked their bikes in the library's bike rack. Then they went inside quickly— almost too quickly. They were so excited to tell Ellen what they had found out that they almost left Wishbone outside.

"Hey! Wait for the dog!" he said, as he quickly dashed through the closing door. Wishbone looked in back of him. "Okay," he said, "the tail is still there."

Ellen was sitting on her stool behind the front counter, chatting with Wanda Gilmore. "Hi!" Ellen and Wanda greeted them as they all approached the front counter.

"Good news! I found all the 1933 microfiche material," Ellen said proudly. "After you told me last night how you found the newspapers at the *Chronicle,* I decided to run another check here today. And I located a mislabeled folder—the 1933 microfiche."

"We have some news for you, too," Sam told Mrs. Talbot. Joe, Sam, and David described their visit to Mr. Groves. They told of how he backed up everything Giles Gilmore wrote in the *Chronicle.*

"I knew that Dad wouldn't make up such serious accusations," Wanda said.

As the kids continued to tell the story about their meeting with Groves, Wishbone looked around the library. It didn't seem to be a very busy day. There weren't many people there. But Wishbone noticed that Mr. Carroll was again sitting at his favorite reading table. He was surrounded by what seemed to be the same amount of books he always had in front of him. *I will have to lie low. I'm not sure he likes dogs.*

Wishbone was worried when Mr. Carroll looked over at him. It seemed that Wishbone's days of being allowed in the library might be numbered. One complaint from Mr. Carroll, and the dog would be out of there for good.

"So someone was deliberately trying to hide those articles about the cancellation of the parade for the Oaks?" Ellen asked.

"I think so," Joe replied. "I also think the same

person knew we were getting close to finding out what happened back in 1933. Whoever it was also must have stolen the first edition of the history book so we couldn't use it for clues."

"So we know *what* that person was trying to hide," David added. "But we still don't really know *who* or *why*."

"Where do we go from here?" Sam asked, puzzled.

"I think we need to find out who was on the town council in 1933," Joe said. "Where would we look for that information, Mom?" he asked Ellen.

"There will be an article written in the *Chronicle* about that year's council elections," Wanda said. "I can help you find it."

Ellen and Wanda disappeared into the main office. In a few moments they came back out with another small microfiche folder. Everyone followed Wanda to the microfiche machine. She sat down and efficiently began to search for the election results.

"Here they are," Wanda said. Everyone leaned in to get a closer look as she read the names aloud. "Jonathan Hale, William Brooks, Jim Mills, Dr. Allen Carroll, Alexander—"

Joe interrupted her. "Wait a minute! Dr. Allen Carroll?" Everyone slowly looked at one another.

"What?" Wanda asked, confused. "What is it?"

"I wonder if he's related to—" Joe began.

"To me?" A voice behind them finished Joe's sentence.

"Whoa! Hey! Look out!" Wishbone cried out as he quickly spun around.

The voice was that of the man who had been a steady fixture in the Henderson Memorial Library ever since they had started to investigate the mystery. The voice belonged to Mr. Carroll.

"Mr. Carroll?" Ellen asked, puzzled.

"I'm afraid I'm the one you're looking for," the thin man said.

"You are behind all the missing materials?" Wanda asked, rising from her seat.

"Why, Mr. Carroll?" Sam asked.

"You see, kids," Mr. Carroll said, nervously scratching the back of his head, "as you discovered, my father was on the town council in 1933. He was one of the council members who came up with the plan to cancel the parade for the baseball team."

Everyone stared in silent disbelief.

Mr. Carroll continued with his explanation. "I actually discovered Mr. Gilmore's articles a few years ago, when I started to do research on my family's history."

Mr. Carroll leaned against a nearby magazine rack. He let out a sigh, then continued.

"My father had already passed away, so I asked my mother, who was still alive then, about what had happened all those years ago. From what I overheard of your conversation, she told me the same thing that Mr. Groves told you. She told me that everything written about the incident in the *Chronicle* was true. But what she also told me was that my father had become ashamed later in his life for what he did."

Mr. Carroll paused. Wishbone saw everyone silently looking at one another in disbelief.

"Kids, my father really was a good man," Mr. Carroll continued. "He had some ways of thinking that seem terrible today. He also made some bad mistakes, especially like the one he made when the Oakdale Oaks won the national championship. But he had also done a lot of good in his lifetime. Unfortunately, history often doesn't remember you for the good you've done, but only for the bad."

Mr. Carroll paused and took in a deep breath before continuing with his own confession of guilt.

"So I'm the one who hid all the newspapers, both here and at the *Chronicle*. I would've just taken the issues with the Gilmore articles in them, but I thought an entire missing year's worth of papers would make it look more like a filing mistake. My research into my family history gave me easy access to both the microfiche documents and the original newspapers."

Wanda stepped forward. "I realize how much you wanted to protect your father's reputation. I myself have been in the same situation with my dad. But that's no excuse to hide the truth, or to deny the community of an entire year of Oakdale's history, Mr. Carroll!"

"I'm sorry, Miss Gilmore," the man replied. "I suppose I thought that getting rid of the articles would have erased what happened, and what my father did." He took in a deep breath. "But from what I've been overhearing about the people you've talked to, I don't suppose that's true."

"What about the first edition of the Oakdale history book?" Joe asked.

"There was a big section in that edition about the Oaks, and about the parade scandal. I checked the later editions, but it seemed that the entire portion about the scandal had been edited out. I guess I wasn't the only person who thought about getting rid of the town's shameful history. But don't worry," Mr. Carroll added, "I'll go get it for you. I hid it in the cooking section."

Wishbone's ears perked up. "Now, that was a mistake," the little dog said. "I'm sure I would have sniffed it out of that section sooner or later."

Joe couldn't believe it! The mystery had finally been solved! Mr. Carroll had hidden the newspapers and the history book in order to save his father's reputation. One thing was for sure, though—Joe could definitely relate to Mr. Carroll's feelings for his father. Joe knew he could never do such a thing to protect his father if his father had ever done anything so wrong.

But if Joe were in Mr. Carroll's shoes, he certainly might have been tempted.

Joe suddenly realized that Mr. Carroll had been flushed out just like Jonas Oldacre, the Norwood builder and supposed murder victim from Sherlock Holmes's short story. Holmes knew that Oldacre must have been hiding somewhere inside the house.

So the great detective had a few of the local police yell "Fire!" after Holmes had set a small, but harmless, fire. Jonas Oldacre came rushing out of his secret room and was caught on the spot. As it turned out, the young lawyer, John McFarlane, was cleared of the crime, since there wasn't a murder in the first place. Holmes learned that Jonas Oldacre had faked his own murder in order to get out of debt!

Joe's thoughts came back to the present situation as Mr. Carroll turned to the group and spoke. "I'm very sorry," he said. "I guess I shouldn't have interfered. I should have just let history speak for itself and be the judge of my father. I regret all the hard work you did while trying to find the missing newspapers," Mr. Carroll said. "I wish I could make it up to you somehow."

Suddenly, Joe came up with an idea. "I can think of something," Joe said. "And it just may help—a little bit, anyway."

Chapter Twelve

"Hello? Mr. Horton?" Wishbone heard Joe speak into the kitchen telephone. "My name is Joe Talbot, and I'm calling from Oakdale."

"Oakdale again?!" Even though the receiver was pressed against Joe's ear, Wishbone could hear the angry man's reply.

"Please don't hang up, sir," Joe said as quickly as he could get the words out of his mouth. "I have an idea that I want to suggest to you."

Wishbone left the kitchen and trotted into the study. Once there, he crawled until he was halfway under his big red chair. When he slowly backed out, he had the baseball that Lindsay Groves had given him earlier that day. He set the ball down in front of him and gave it a good sniffing.

"Nope, the chair didn't give it the seasoning I was hoping for. It looks like you need a trip to Wanda's yard," Wishbone said. "Besides, it's time to set a trap for one burglar!"

The terrier grabbed the baseball in his teeth. He took off through the kitchen and out his doggie door.

Once again, Wishbone carefully crept into Wanda's dark yard. He was on a mission to bury a treasure. He sniffed out a nice, soft spot in the middle of the yard. Then he set down the baseball and began to dig. When the hole was the right depth, he grabbed the ball and dropped it in. Dirt flew between his legs as he filled the fresh hole. After taking a couple of quick looks around, Wishbone took off to some nearby bushes. This time, he had a plan.

After a few minutes of waiting, a small scratching noise directed his attention to the wooden fence in Wanda's backyard. At the top of the fence, he saw two handlike paws appear. They were soon followed by a gray-and-black furry animal. He saw the creature hoist its way to the top of the fence, pause, then slide down the other side into the yard. It landed on the ground with a small thud. The strange animal shook the dirt off its coat and then looked around.

Once the creature was on the ground, Wishbone could get a good look at what it actually was. It was completely gray, except for black rings that circled its long, bushy tail. A black stripe seemed to cross right over its face, just like a mask. Why, it was a raccoon!

Wishbone quietly put his nose to the air and took in a small sniff. Luckily, the wind was coming from the direction of the raccoon, and not blowing from Wishbone's direction. That way, he could pick up the visitor's scent, and not the other way around. Into his nose floated a scent that had become familiar to him only recently. *"That's* what that strange smell was!" he whispered to himself. "Raccoon smell," the dog said, naming the recently discovered scent. "I'll have to remember that."

Wishbone watched as the raccoon made its way toward the freshly covered hole. He gave the fresh mound of dirt a couple of sniffs. Then he began to dig. After a while, the raccoon stopped digging. His back half stuck out of the hole as his ringed tail flicked back and forth. Slowly, the gray fur ball backed out of the hole. To Wishbone's alarm, the animal was carrying the freshly buried baseball. The raccoon carefully inspected the newfound treasure, turning it over in its little black hands. Wishbone then watched the trespasser as it brought the ball it its nose, sniffed, then went ahead and took a bite.

"Whoa!" Wishbone whispered. "I'm the only one that's supposed to be chewing on that thing!"

Seeing that the baseball wasn't some form of food, the raccoon casually dropped it back into the hole. Then it began to sniff around the rest of the yard. It walked toward the bushes that Wishbone was hiding behind. Just before it reached them, it caught a whiff of another buried object and then started to dig once more.

That was Wishbone's chance! It was time to call an end to this little bandit's escapades! Wishbone leaped over the bushes and landed right in front of the digging raccoon.

"Hooooooooo-whacha!"

Wishbone found himself standing nose to nose with the furry gray robber. For a moment, neither

119

animal moved. The two just stood there staring at each other.

"*O-kaaaaaaaay* . . ." Wishbone said. "*Now* what do I do?"

A bright light suddenly shone on Wishbone, causing him to see nothing but big white spots for a few moments. Then he turned to find the source of the harsh light. He saw Wanda Gilmore—at least he thought it was Wanda. The lady holding the flashlight was wearing a robe and had green guacamole all over her face—at least, that was what it looked like to Wishbone.

"Wishbone!" the lady said loudly. "What are you up to?!"

Yep, that's Wanda, Wishbone thought. He turned back to face the intruder. The raccoon was just scurrying up one side of the back fence. Then he quickly disappeared on the other side.

"And let that be a lesson to you!" Wishbone barked to the retreating raccoon. He turned toward Wanda. "Did you see that?" he asked. "I scared him off for you!"

Wanda's flashlight beam moved back and forth from Wishbone to the one and a half open holes in her backyard. "Oh, Wishbone!" she said angrily. "What have you done?!"

"But, Wanda," the little dog said, backing up slowly, "it wasn't me . . . not this time, anyway!" Wishbone ran to the back fence and barked. "Didn't you see him?" he asked. "I mean . . . he was the one wearing the mask!"

"Wishbone!" Wanda said in a deep and upset tone, her voice cracking a bit.

"Uh . . . good night, Wanda. I'll come back and we can chat when you're in a better mood—like maybe next month!" Wishbone said. He raced for the safety of his doggie door.

Lying in bed, Joe saw Wishbone run into the bedroom and dive under the bed. "What's wrong, boy?" Joe asked, as he moved his hand over the side of the bed. The little dog gave it a couple of licks, but he remained in hiding. Joe hoped the dog wasn't in trouble with Wanda again.

Usually when Wishbone hid under the bed like that, Wanda was at the Talbots' door a moment later. Joe rolled over and picked up his clock. It was already quite late. Wanda probably wouldn't show up tonight. Joe dropped his hand down again. This time, Wishbone crawled out from under the bed just far enough for Joe to be able to scratch behind his ears.

Joe imagined he could hear Wishbone saying, "If a tall, thin, auburn-haired lady comes looking for me, you haven't seen me, okay?" Joe laughed to himself.

Reaching over to his bedside nightstand once more, Joe picked up his two Oakdale Oaks baseball cards. He carefully removed them from their protective sleeves and stared at them. Occasionally, he turned them over in his hands. He could see Lindsay Groves's new signature on his card. The ballplayer had been happy to sign it when Joe had asked.

Looking at the two cards, Joe tried to imagine himself back in a time when racial prejudice would cause an entirely different baseball league to come into being. He tried hard, but he found the idea impossible to understand.

He considered himself lucky to be living in a place, and in a time, where that didn't happen. At least, he was in a place where it wasn't supposed to happen. But from what he'd learned during the past couple of days, he had been wrong about Oakdale.

Joe got out of bed and went over to his bookcase. He removed the scrapbook that contained his father's collection. Wishbone slowly came out from under the bed and hopped on top of it. Joe got back into bed with the scrapbook and opened it to a blank page. On the page were several empty card-sized slots. Joe carefully placed the two Oaks cards into two of the slots. He turned the page and gazed at the old Oaks program that was inside its own bound sleeve. Then Joe slowly turned the pages back toward the beginning of the collection. He inspected his father's original cards, and the new ones from Mrs. McKinley's husband's collection.

Finally, after closing the book, Joe got up and returned it to the bookshelf. He climbed back into bed and slowly slid his feet under the blanket. Wishbone circled a couple of times, then lay down beside him.

Chapter Thirteen

Two weeks later, the sun shone brightly on Oak Street. To Joe, it seemed as if everyone who lived in Oakdale was present. Joe was standing on the curb in front of Pepper Pete's. Next to him were David, Sam, his mom, and Mr. Carroll. Wishbone sat in front of Joe, tail wagging at all the excitement.

Joe looked around and gazed at the people lining each side of the street as far as he could see. He saw Dr. Brown a few yards away. She saw him and waved. He waved back. Above them, stretched across the street from Beck's Grocery to Rosie's Rendezvous, was a banner that read: OAKDALE FOUNDER'S DAY. The sign flapped in the breeze. The air was filled with music as the high-school band marched down the street.

"Look!" Sam said, pointing up the street. "Here they come!"

Coming slowly down the street was Wanda's antique white Thunderbird, with its top down. She was driving and waving. The maroon and yellow ribbons draped over the sides of her car fluttered in the breeze.

Sitting on the back of the car, waving to the crowd, was Lindsay Groves and his great-grandson Joshua. Mr. Groves was dressed in his original Oakdale Oaks baseball uniform. Joshua was wearing a Little League uniform. Mr. Groves was even wearing his old baseball glove. On the side of the car, a sign read: LINDSAY GROVES—RELIEF PITCHER FOR THE OAKDALE OAKS, NEGRO LEAGUE NATIONAL CHAMPS, 1933.

Behind them, other convertibles slowly followed. Each of them carried surviving Oaks team members or their descendants. Some wore baseball uniforms; others held bats or gloves. All of them looked happy as they waved to the crowd.

Joe got a great view of the car carrying Wesley Horton, grandson of Ron Horton, the Oakdale Oaks shortstop. The young man was dressed in jeans and an old Oaks shirt.

Joe realized that it had taken more than sixty years, but the Oakdale Oaks had finally gotten their victory parade.

"Thanks for asking the town council to do this, Mr. Carroll," Sam said.

"Yes," Joe agreed. "This is really great!"

"I should be thanking you kids," Mr. Carroll replied. "It was your idea. You are the ones who helped me right my father's wrong."

Joe was about to reply when David got everyone's attention. "Look!" he said, pointing up the street.

Joe looked up the street and was very excited by what he saw. Slowly making its way toward them was a huge float commemorating the Negro League. Standing on a large green base were three giant papier-mâché figures. The one closest to them was kneeling and had his back to them. In front of that figure stood another. That one was standing sideways, holding a large baseball bat over one shoulder. At the other end of the float stood the third figure on a small mound. With a glove on one hand and a ball in the other, he was rearing back for the pitch. This third figure resembled the photograph of Lindsay Groves that accompanied the interview Joe had found in the *Chronicle*.

As the float passed them, Joe got a good look at the sign on its side: IN HONOR OF ALL PLAYERS OF THE NEGRO LEAGUE.

As the float passed, Sam turned and smiled at Joe, David, and Mr. Carroll. "The float was really a great idea, Mr. Carroll," she said. "I think it adds the perfect touch to the parade."

"It was the least I could do," he replied. "But if you will excuse me, there are a few more things I need to do." Mr. Carroll made his way through the crowd, following the parade route.

The Negro League float was the last part of the parade. After it passed, the crowd slowly made its way into the street. Sam, Joe, David, Ellen, and Wishbone did the same. Everyone seemed to be making their way to a small wooden stage that had been built in the vacant lot next to Beck's Grocery.

On the stage itself, on the right side, several people Sam recognized as current Oakdale town council members sat in two short rows of folding chairs. Slowly taking their seats on the opposite side of the stage were the surviving members of the Oakdale Oaks and their descendants. As Lindsay Groves saw the kids in the crowd, he smiled and he gave them a quick wave. They each waved back.

Once everybody seemed to be in place, Mr. Carroll stepped up to a small podium at the center of the stage. As he stood there, the crowd slowly fell silent. He took in a deep breath and began his speech. "Friends and citizens of Oakdale, welcome to this year's Founder's Day celebration. My name is Joseph Carroll. My father, Dr. Allen Carroll, sat on Oakdale's town council many years ago."

He gestured to the group of people on his left.

"I asked the current town council members if I could make a short speech this year in honor of some very special Oakdale heroes—some forgotten heroes."

He took in another deep breath, then continued. "Many of you may not have known about the Oakdale Oaks until recently, when Founder's Day was advertised in the paper and on the radio. They were a fine team of the Negro Baseball League. If a few of you do remember the Oaks, you may even remember that they won the national championship in 1933. But those of you who do remember that may not be familiar with what happened soon afterward.

"You see, they were promised a victory parade down Oak Street here. But they never got it—until today, that is. My father and some of the other council members of that time canceled the parade because of what they called 'zoning restrictions.'" Mr. Carroll paused and looked around at the crowd. "Unfortunately, they really canceled the parade because of the color of the team members' skin."

There was murmuring in the crowd as those too young to remember took in the surprising information.

Mr. Carroll went on. "My father's racial prejudice and the decision to cancel the parade were mistakes my father deeply regretted until the very end of his life. Though he never knew about the pain he had caused the Oaks, he suffered in his own way because of his own prejudice."

Mr. Carroll quickly brushed a hand across one eye. He cleared his throat, then continued.

"I, too, share in my father's regret. I tried to hide what my father had done. I tried to rub out that ugly episode of our local history. But, in the end, I couldn't. No one can erase such a thing. You see, no matter how many history books are changed, and no matter how much people try to cover up the truth, you can't go back in time and change what really happened. You can't go back and change how the past affected real people."

Mr. Carroll turned to the Oaks and their relatives.

"I know I can't change what happened to you those many years ago."

Then he turned back to face the crowd.

"But we can honor these forgotten heroes here today."

He picked up a plaque that was resting on the podium. Mr. Carroll turned it so the front was facing him.

"I want to read to you what's written on this plaque. It says: 'On this field played the 1933 national champs—the Oakdale Oaks. Remember them with pride.'"

Mr. Carroll set the plaque back down onto the podium.

"I would like to announce that, with help from the Oakdale Historical Society . . ."—he paused, looked at Wanda, and smiled—"this plaque will be placed at what will soon be the fully restored Legion Field, the home of the Oakdale Oaks!"

This was a complete surprise to Sam, Joe, and David. Along with the rest of the audience, they began to applaud. Mr. Carroll put up his hands, and the clapping died down before it could gain momentum.

Turning back to the Oaks and their family members, Mr. Carroll continued. "So, on behalf of my late father and all of Oakdale, I deeply apologize. I only hope it's not too late."

Slowly, Sam watched as Lindsay Groves got to his feet and made his way toward the podium at the center of the stage. The audience was completely quiet as Mr.

Carroll stepped aside and Mr. Groves took his place at the podium.

"I must say," he began, "that I didn't think I would ever find myself back in Oakdale, not to mention riding in a parade through downtown. But I just wanted to give thanks to some other people who helped make this possible." Lindsay Groves pointed toward the kids. "Joe Talbot, Samantha Kepler, and David Barnes."

Down by her feet, Sam heard a gruff bark. She looked down to see Wishbone standing on his hind legs.

Mr. Groves must have seen him, as well. "Oh, yes, and Mr. Wishbone, there." The crowd gave a small laugh as the old ball player continued. "These kids played a big part in bringing us here today. They're prime examples of how we as a society can eventually and completely overcome our problems."

Lindsay Groves turned toward Mr. Carroll.

"And, as for your apology, Mr. Carroll . . ." As Groves paused, a brief, uncomfortable tension filled the air. Lindsay Groves looked back at the retired players and their families, then back at Mr. Carroll. He continued: "On behalf of the Oakdale Oaks and their descendants, your apology is accepted."

He extended his right hand to Mr. Carroll, and Mr. Carroll took Groves's hand in both of his. Mr. Carroll smiled broadly as he shook hands with the former ball player. The audience broke out in a symphony of cheers and applause as the rest of the players and their relatives stood and followed Groves's hand-shaking ceremony. The council members followed.

Soon, the entire stage was full of people shaking each other's hands.

Sam was happy for the Oakdale Oaks, who finally got their parade. The mystery had been solved, and everything had worked out for everybody.

She looked over at Joe and David. Joe was smiling as he looked up at the stage. David was smiling, as well, but it looked as if his was only a half-smile. David was still upset about what they had discovered about their hometown.

Sam didn't know if David had ever faced the kind of issues they had uncovered recently. Living in the same Oakdale where she did, she thought he probably hadn't. Sam wished there was something she could do or say to make David feel better. But she knew this was something David would have to work out for himself.

"Ladies and gentlemen," Mr. Carroll announced into the microphone on the podium. "I'd now like you to join us at Legion Field as we round out our Founder's Day celebration with a softball game!"

David popped his kickstand down with his foot and leaned his bike against it. He looked around to see Legion Field more alive than he'd ever seen it before. The crowd was slowly beginning to file in and fill the bleachers. The field itself was also beginning to show signs of Mr. Carroll's renovation. The tall weeds were gone, and many of the old bleacher seats had been replaced with new planks of smooth lumber. David saw that the back wall even had some new sections added. Thanks to Mr. Carroll, it appeared Legion Field was well on its way to its original appearance.

David, Sam, and Joe walked toward the stands. Ellen and Wanda were helping at the concession stand. Wishbone trotted in front, his nose lifted into the air to catch all of the passing smells.

As they got close to the diamond itself, David looked to the bleachers and saw a special section marked off for the Oakdale Oaks. Sitting in that area, Lindsay Groves waved the kids over.

"Kids!" the former relief pitcher called out. "I want you to meet some friends of mine." As the kids approached, four other gray-haired men stood up from the bleachers. Lindsay Groves continued. "Sam, Joe, David"—he looked down to the dog at his feet—"and Mr. Wishbone, I know you might have talked to a couple of these characters over the phone, but I want you to meet them in person."

Mr. Groves turned to the other men.

"This, here, is John 'Bullet' Foster, Sam 'The Dog' Johnson, 'Sluggin' Tom Wilson, and Weldon 'Smokin' Greer."

Each of the men tipped their baseball caps toward the kids and Wishbone.

Sam "The Dog" Johnson, a short, heavyset man, leaned forward toward Wishbone and tipped his white ball cap again. "I'm a dog just like you, Mr. Wishbone. What do think about that?" The four men laughed as Wishbone reared back on his haunches and pawed the air.

Lindsay Groves leaned down to Wishbone. He

placed his hand in front of his mouth, as if he were telling a secret. He said, "They called him 'The Dog' because his bark was worse than his bite."

Everyone laughed.

"What was your nickname, Mr. Groves?" Joe asked.

Weldon Greer, a thin man wearing an old Oaks baseball shirt and thick, horn-rimmed glasses, spoke up. "We used to call him 'Slick,' because that man could slide the ball past anyone—anyone except me, of course."

As the men laughed and joked with one another, it was easy for David to imagine them very young and in the prime of their baseball careers.

"We want to thank you kids for all you've done," John "Bullet" Foster said. His curly gray hair extended down the sides of his face to form a neat beard. He, too, wore an Oaks shirt. "It sure has been good to see the old field and some of our teammates again."

"We couldn't have done it without Mr. Groves," Joe replied.

"I'm sorry we were so rude to you originally on the phone," "Sluggin'" Tom Wilson added. He was the only one of the four former Oaks who was dressed in a suit and tie. If it wasn't for the baseball cap on his head, he would have looked more like a schoolteacher than a former ball player.

"It's a good thing you got old Slick, here, to make a few calls, as well," Sam "The Dog" Johnson added, pointing to Lindsay Groves. "People like 'Bullet' over there can be as stubborn as mules!"

"Hey!" John Foster replied in a mock angry tone. The other four men laughed.

"Well, kids," Mr. Groves said, "I've got one more pitch to make." As he started to edge his way out of the bleachers, David noticed the large softball in his hand. "They've asked me to throw out the first ball."

"Do you think you have any pepper left?" asked "Sluggin" Tom.

"Probably nothing but salt now!" Weldon "Smokin" Greer replied. The four men laughed again.

The kids accompanied Mr. Groves as he walked toward the field. Slowly, Lindsay Groves fell back until it was just him and David walking side by side. He put a hand on David's arm, stopping him.

"What's bothering you, David?" the old man asked. "Is this whole thing not sitting right in your mind?"

"Aren't you angry about the way you were treated back then?" David asked him. "You weren't allowed to have a parade. You weren't allowed to play in the professional leagues. . . ."

"We weren't allowed to eat in the same restaurants. We weren't allowed to use the same water fountains," Lindsay Groves continued for him. "There were lots of things we weren't allowed to do. Of course I was angry. I was angry about every one of those injustices. They weren't fair." He put a hand on David's shoulder. "But, however unfair and unfortunate the situation was, that's the way things were back then. But look at us now. Look where we are. And look how far we're going!"

Groves and David slowly began walking toward the field again. "You have to remember, David," the old man continued, "all those things happened in the past. Now, you and I both know that we should learn from the past and not repeat its mistakes. But more important, we should concern ourselves with the present. We shouldn't hold grudges for the actions of people who lived long ago. It's the actions of people today that are important. And remember, Oakdale has come to terms with its past today. The truth is out, and this will be a better place because of it."

Lindsay Groves stopped David once more.

"I'll let you in on a secret, David. When the council said we couldn't have our parade, I was very upset. That was one thing I was really looking forward to. But, you know what? Looking back, that parade wouldn't have meant half as much as the one today did."

That made David begin to feel better.

Lindsay Groves said, "You see, it was the actions of people today"—he pointed a finger to David's chest—"that have shown me how far society has come. And with society in the hands of kids like you, the world is going to become a very nice place to live in. . . ."

Lindsay Groves was interrupted by the announcement of his name over the field's public-address system.

He turned to David just before entering the infield and said, "And it's going to be a nice place to play baseball in, too!"

The crowd in the stands applauded as Groves walked onto the field. Feeling better, David joined the crowd in their applause.

Wishbone watched as Lindsay Groves took to the field. His tail wagged as Groves stepped onto the pitcher's mound. He lightly threw the large softball to the catcher. Wishbone planted his feet firmly into the ground as he quickly stopped an urge to go chase after the flying softball.

As the ball landed snugly inside the catcher's glove, the onlookers filling the stands roared with cheers. Everyone got up and gave Groves a standing ovation. He took off his cap and waved a thank-you to the crowd as he walked off the field. Wishbone saw the old ball player's eyes fill with tears. It seemed this day really did mean a lot to him.

Wishbone looked all around Legion Field. He wasn't used to seeing it so alive with people. Every time he had gone there with Joe, the place was almost like an old ghost town. Now, Wishbone thought, it probably looked close to what Lindsay Groves saw when he looked into the stands years ago as a young player.

Wishbone looked back onto the field to see Sam at first base, and David at second. His buddy, Joe, was occupying Wishbone's usual spot in center field. "Go get 'em, Joe!" Wishbone barked to the field. He wished he could be out there chasing balls.

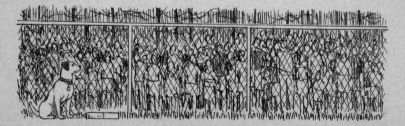

The little dog turned toward the bleachers. But, then again, it wouldn't be long before he was out there with Joe, Sam, and David again. Suddenly, a familiar smell blew past Wishbone's nose. He ran toward the stands.

"Right now," he said, his tail wagging with excitement, "I'm going to show everybody what baseball is really about!" As he reached the stands, Wishbone cocked an ear and listened for those two magic words.

In the distance, at the other end of a row of bleachers, a loud voice yelled, "Hot dogs! Get your hot dogs!"

Wishbone took off toward the man carrying a large box of steamed, ballpark hot dogs.

"At least, that's what baseball is really all about for me!"

About Michael Anthony Steele

Michael Anthony Steele—or Ant, as he is known to his friends—loves mysteries and is no stranger to writing for dogs. In fact, when he was growing up on his family's farm in East Texas, he would often write for his hound dog, Duke.

As Duke placed himself in certain situations, Ant would put phrases into his dog's mouth, such as, "Please, just one more piece of food and I won't ever beg again," or, "But cows are fun to bark at," or, "But, I thought you would like this smell! That's why I rolled in it!" Sometimes finding out what Duke had rolled in could be quite a mystery in itself.

Ant's first experience with Wishbone was during the first season of the TV show. He worked as a prop assistant under the expert guidance of prop master Tom Rutherford. By the way, a prop is any object used by an actor, such as a sword, pen, cup, etc. Ant helped build and buy many of the props used by the actors on the show, or even those used by Wishbone himself.

During the filming, Ant answered his calling as an author by taking the time to write and submit two scripts. He submitted them to the show's producers, hoping they would like his work. They did. When the next TV season began, Ant was hired as a staff writer. He got the opportunity to co-write the one-hour Halloween special, *Halloween Hound: The Legend of*

Creepy Collars; the TV episode *War of the Noses*; and Wishbone's first movie, *WISHBONE's Dog Days of the West*.

Currently, Ant lives in Plano, Texas, with his wife, Becky, and a house full of animals. They have two Chihuahuas, named Juno and Echo; and an English bulldog, named Rufus. They also have two Siamese cats, named Pluto and Bromius; a snake named Bishop; and an aviary full of finches and canaries. Wishbone would approve of the dogs, snake, and birds, but be sure not to tell him about the cats.

The Adventures of WISHBONE™

Read all the books in
The Adventures of Wishbone™ series!

Read all the books in the
WISHBONE™ Mysteries series!

SHARE THE ADVENTURE! SOLVE THE MYSTERIES!

JOIN THE
WISHBONE ZONE
FAN CLUB

Don't miss an exciting and fun-filled issue of *The WISHBONE™ ZONE News!*
Send in your order form today!

For only $10 for a one-year membership, **WISHBONE ZONE** members who enroll or renew during 1999 will receive:

- Authentic **WISHBONE** Dog Tag like the one **Wishbone™** wears! This is an exclusive item for **WISHBONE ZONE** members only! Not available for sale—anywhere!
- One-year subscription to *The WISHBONE ZONE News*—That's at least four issues of the hottest newsletter around!
- Special edition of **The Adventures of Wishbone** mini-book *Tail of Terror*
- **WISHBONE** Dog Days of the West photocard
- Photo of **Wishbone** and the cast
- **WISHBONE** bookmark
- **WISHBONE** poster

KEEP WISHBONE COMING TO YOUR HOME FOR A YEAR!

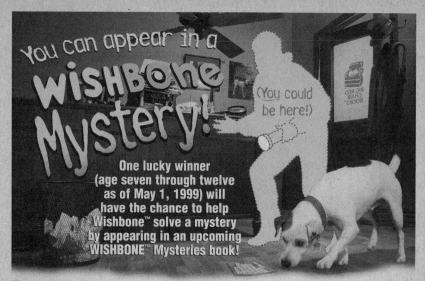